PLAYFUL GESTURES

A NOVEL BY: BERTRAND E. BROWN

Chapter 1

Sylvia sat on the plush loveseat, legs curled underneath her, a cup of hot cocoa by her side on the tiny mahogany end table. The fireplace was lit and emitted a warmth that relaxed her and the idea that Anthony had called letting her know that he was on his way home only made her that much warmer and more secure.

They'd only been married a little over three years but it seemed like a lifetime. He was all that she could have ever wanted and her only concern was if she were enough for him.

She knew women. She had girlfriends who treated their men like stepchildren, and whose men were only in their lives to service them. And for some reason, which she had yet come to understand the men stayed loyal. Sylvia often wondered why these men stayed but who was she to question their motives. Her only concern was taking care of Anthony and making sure she was the best wife a husband could ever ask for and after three years of marriage she must have been doing alright because he was still singing her praises despite the twenty pounds she gained around her midsection and the growing cellulite that had made itself at home on her ass and thighs. The thought brought a small grin to Sylvia's face as she put both the cigarette and glass of wine down on the end table. If anything she knew how her man should and needed to be treated and was good at it and with that thought she placed the book down and went upstairs to the bathroom and started her evening shower. Disrobing slowly she thought of her husband with his smooth silky self and immediately found her nipples grow erect as she eased into the bathtub beneath the steaming hot flow of the shower. As her body adjusted to the warm flow of the water she closed her eyes and smiled.

Anthony's favorite casserole was in the oven on three fifty and the wine was chilling just waiting for his arrival. He'd be famished when he arrived. And after grabbing her, kissing her deeply, passionately and inquiring about her day he'd sit down to dinner and eat with great gusto before leaning back in his chair unloosening his pants and picking up the evening paper and scouring over the sports section.

After staring at a laptop all day he welcomed glancing at the box scores in the evening paper. It had almost become a daily ritual by this time and Sylvia had not only accepted it but also embraced it. She realized the importance of giving him his space and allowing him to unwind after a long day at the brokerage firm of Mitchell and Ness where he spent eight arduous hours a day in the throes of other people's money brokering to make the most of others assets. It was a thoughtless job and he never considered the negatives as a business and finance student while at Yale but after ten years at the firm he realized that life was about more than just acquiring assets. He'd built quite a portfolio in those ten years but as Sylvia knew Anthony had long since lost any reward or satisfaction in his career choice. The couple had gotten married and for the first time since joining the firm Anthony felt that his life had been rejuvenated. Sylvia invigorated him and gave him a sense of life that had more or less evaporated in the past couple of years. She was the consummate woman, handling the finances with ease, always making the right decisions and she was an extraordinary cook. Bright, she kept him abreast of all the news with her insightful twist on the latest politics and seemed to have the inside scoop on the celebrity news as well. In bed he hadn't met her equal and she took him to heights he'd never known before and if there was a factor that did more than anything to sway him to even consider marriage this was probably the biggest factor.

Being a single Black man in New York he knew he was one of only a small handful of brothas down on Wall Street with a major brokerage firm. It hadn't taken him long to hit six figures and it wasn't long before the firm and his clients came to realize why he had been so highly recruited. Still, in virtually no time at all he grew tired of the madness that surrounded Wall Street.

At first, every one saw him as a natural, and he quickly gained a reputation for his proficiency not only with his buying and selling of stock but also in the night life that accompanied up and coming young brokers. Young women with aspirations of luring one of these six figure players were plentiful and frequented the clubs that surrounded the brokerage houses and Anthony always on the prowl was more than a hot commodity. His reputation preceding him he welcomed the company and after procuring a Manhattan loft overlooking the East River he entertained the ladies on a regular basis but this too soon became mundane and he quickly became tired of the game and resigned himself to curling up with a good book, some smooth jazz and a glass of whatever he desired. That was until he met Sylvia at the bookstore down on West 4th. At first her thick thighs, shapely legs and dimples that accentuated her chocolate mocha skin and smile had taken him. But after listening to her conversate with the bookstore owner he knew that she had all the qualities he relished in a woman. Not long after that they started dating and he was pleasantly surprised to find out that she was not only a teacher but also quite a proficient one. Soon thereafter he had taken her home to his parents who not only fell in love with her but insisted on her accompanying them to the Bahamas where they had a piece of a time share That pretty much made and cemented the decision for him and not long after that they'd been married. The marriage was now in its third year was so much more than he could have ever dreamed of and after moving across the river to Jersey they decided to start a family. Anthony had to constantly check himself and more often than even he would have liked to admit he would stare at this woman, his wife, and try to figure out what kept him so intrigued. His past relationships, even the one's he considered durable and stable seldom lasted no more than a couple of months no matter how bright and beautiful the woman to be. But as intense as he was he would quickly come to bleed her of all cerebral matter and become somehow disenchanted.

That had hardly been the case where Sylvia was concerned and that was not to say that the two did not have their difficulties. She was as strong willed and passionate about her principles and convictions as he was and there skirmishes which often turned to battles and then all-out war would sometimes last for weeks before he would ultimately concede and make the peace. Still, whenever he'd envision marriage he had never seen the upside having always believed that men were essentially polygamous as opposed to women who were basically monogamous. The thought of marriage use to make him break out in cold sweats but after four years he had fallen in line and often times had to check his man card to see if he was still a card carrying member. The reality of it all was he was just about as spoiled as he'd been in his parent's household. And whereas all the fly-by-night dates were always more concerned with their own concerns than they were with him and simply looked at him as a potential meal ticket. But not Sylvia who was as free and independent as he was but still had the wherewithal to cater to his every need despite having a life independent and just as active as his. Seeing this he was adamant about giving her everything she could imagine as well making for quite the happy couple.

Several years Anthony's senior and her childbearing years coming quickly to a close she hadn't given children thought until Anthony had started made it a more and more frequent topic of conversation. Sylvia had never particularly had a desire to have children after years wiping snotty nosed brats' noses in the classroom and she was quite content to leave the childrearing to someone else.

Her career gave her all the contact with children she felt she would ever need and she had long ago resigned herself to the fact that she did not want any kids running around pulling at her apron strings. Apron strings? Hell, if it wasn't Michael Kors or Jones of New York she wasn't wearing it let alone some damn apron but if that's what Anthony wanted then she resigned herself to having his children. She'd worked long and hard to maintain her shape and childbirth hadn't exactly been in her plans but she had to admit she did like the practice and so without further ado she resigned herself to the idea of being a prospective mother. And so after dinner she assumed her wifely duties and sat peacefully by the fireplace in her finest evening wear as she did every evening for the past two or three months waiting for her fine, young, husband to finish his meal and his paper and be attentive to her needs. After months of the same, it had almost become ritual by now and though Sylvia loved Anthony she was missing something. The impulsive, spontaneity that had once made this young man so appealing was now a thing of the past and Syl wondered if Ant was feeling as she was and decided that perhaps it was time to try something new, something different. She'd been having these thoughts for more than a week now and when she saw Anthony push his chair from the dining room table and unbuckle his belt she took her cue and finished her drink and doused her cigarette in the glass. Moving forward she let her arms drape around Anthony's neck and pulled his left arm around to the back of the chair, snapping the handcuffs on his wrist and then snapped it to the top bottom rung of the chair. Before Ant could react she'd done the same thing to his other hand. Looking up in surprise, Syl smiled coyly. Realizing he was at his wife's mercy, Ant smiled. He wouldn't have minded but today of all days had been particularly tiring and he was exhausted.

"Baby," he said smiling in appreciation of his wife's initiative and creativity. He relished the fact that he had a woman that would go to any means to please him but tonight he just wasn't in the mood.

"Baby," he repeated. "You know I love you but tonight's just not a good night. I had Mr. Mitchell in my office for half the day going over the Wright proposal," he said half explaining and half pleading.

"I know," Sylvia said. "And I know how Mr. Mitchell can be," as she unbuttoned his shirt, "and that's why mommy is going to take care of her baby tonight," she said zipping his pants down and running her tongue from his neck down to his navel. Ant let his head drop and felt his hair rise. Aroused he moaned as Sylvia reached for the Vaseline and began to stroke him slowly. He felt himself grow and opened his eyes only briefly to see her disrobe in front of him. Her nipples glistened as she pinched them between her fingers and first guided them to her mouth where she licked each gently and then to his mouth.

"Suck them baby," she said continuing to guide them into his mouth.

"Baby," Anthony repeated still pleading and glad that she'd stop stroking him. "You know I love you to death but honestly it's a bad time."

"A bad time," Sylvia smiled. "Well, let me make it better for my baby," she said falling to her knees and taking the full length of his member into her mouth sucking slowly, as she stroked his now rock hard penis with all the love and tenderness she could muster when she felt him begin to tense up and suddenly realizing he was on the verge of coming she released him turned and bent over. Looking up from between her legs she grabbed his still throbbing member and guided into her now dripping pussy, emitting a gasp as she did so.

"Damn baby you feel good," Sitting up she eased down onto him taking as much of him as she could. "Oh shit," she screamed as she eased up and down on his hard dick. "Damn baby." Ant feeling the warm pussy Anthony met her every thrust trying his best to get all of his ten inches up in her. They were moving together, riding the crest of each wave in an ocean of pleasure.

"Oh yeah, fuck me baby. Fuck me good. Fuck me like this is the best pussy you've ever had. Let me come all over your dick. Damn baby! Tell me the pussy's good to you."

"Its good baby," Anthony managed to mutter between clenched teeth.

"Tell me whose dick it is?"

"It's your dick baby," Ant said repeating his wife's words.

"Then give me that come dammit." Syl yelled now on the verge of coming herself.

"I'm going to give it to you baby."

"Give it to me baby. Where do you want to give it to me baby? Do you wanna to come in me baby?" Syl said slowing it down in an attempt to procure an answer.

"You want to come in my mouth baby or do you wanna come in my ass?" Syl slowed her motion down knowing that this kind of talk could make her husband come just as much as her actions. He was ready too. "You want to come in my mouth don'tcha boo?" Ant shook his head.

"Let me taste my pussy," Syl said easing off his throbbing dick and sticking her hand back in the jar of Vaseline grabbed his penis and stroked it slowly gently before gently sucking the tip.

"Oh my God baby take it all. Suck it baby. Suck it hard. Are you gonna swallow me baby?"

"Every drop baby."

Ant threw his head back and tried to grab her head but the handcuffs held tight. At her mercy and half out of his mind. Ant pleaded. "What do you want Syl? Anything baby. Just tell me what you want."

"I want you to come for me baby. Come on sweetie give me that come," Syl said taking all of his long, thick dick and letting it hit the back of her throat and gagging on it but refusing to choke. She knew he loved this and seconds later he erupted shooting long spasms of warm come into her already full mouth. And with each spasm she swallowed until he was void of every drop. When he was empty she continued to suck until he was damn near crying. Spent Sylvia unlocked the cuffs and grabbed Anthony's arm. Ant who had rubbed his wrists raw trying to get away from his wife's attempts to pleasure was now massaging his wrists and allowing her to lead him up the winding staircase and to the master bedroom. When she reached it she crawled up on the bed she pulled him up onto the bed and pulled up the nigh tie exposing her plump round ass. The leopard heels always turned him on and he soon found himself hard again and ready to mount her. Syl dropped her head to the pillow before handing Ant the tiny jar of Vaseline and spreading her cheeks as far apart as she possibly could. Even after their previous tryst she had a hard time taking all of him and she flinched at his initial thrust. By the time it was over both were bathed in sweat and gasping for air.

Falling asleep in each other's arms, legs and arms intertwined Ant wondered how heaven could be any sweeter.

The next day was beautiful. It was May and already the temperatures were in the mid-seventies. He had heard talk about global warming and really didn't understand any more than the next man but if this was global warming then he was all for killing the ozone. If it hadn't been for his weekly meeting with Mr. Mitchell this morning he wouldn't have even bothered going in at all. Sylvia with her ADHD self made all that much easier zooming around the bedroom straightening up and practically making the bed with him still in it. Wouldn't be so damn anxious if she had to go in there and pretend to listen to the same ol'bullshit he'd been listening to for the past ten years.

Convinced that Mitchell enjoyed the sound of his own voice Anthony had long grown tired of the feeble promises of Mr. Mitchell when it came to bringing him in as a partner. At first the thought appealed to him and though his knowledge and expertise far surpassed his peers he somehow found the effort to take it up a notch. At the same time he was steady amassing a portfolio of new ideas and techniques he'd been dwelling over since college that he was sure would take the firm up a peg and turn it into one of the premier brokerage firms in the nation. Of this he was sure but he and Syl after mulling over the idea decided to wait until he was offered a partnership. That was ten years ago and he was still waiting. And every Wednesday for months Syl would call and ask him if Mr. Mitchell had offered him the partnership and every week he would listen to the disappointment in her voice after he told her no. After a while she stopped asking and he stopped hoping until one day during dinner he noticed something was depply troubling her.

"What's on your mind Syl?"

"Nothing really bay. I just had a thought."

"Care to share?"

"Really it was nothing. I just had a thought is all."

Anthony laughed. A few years ago, he may have dismissed it as her having nothing more than cramps but after three years he'd come to know his wife and knew now that something was on her mind and it wasn't something that was just a passing thought. No, from the deep furrow in her brow he could tell that there was something really bothering her.

"Talk to me baby. You know you can't hide anything from me," Ant chuckled. "You're like my twin that was separated at birth. I can hear you; feel your pain even when you're not around. Talk to me sweetheart. You know you can't keep anything from me. If something's bothering you let it out. If you can't tell me who can you tell?"

Syl dropped her head.

"C'mon baby. There have never been any secrets between us."

"You're right."

"I know I'm right so talk to me," Anthony said his anger mounting. "Want another glass of wine?" He said reaching for the bottle and pouring himself a half a glass before changing his mind and getting up and grabbing aclean glass and the bottle of Chivas Regal. Pouring himself a double that verged on the cusp of being a triple he offered the bottle to his comely wife who nodded no to his overtures. Taking a long sip that damn near drained the glass he poured another before sitting back down.

"Okay, are you ready to tell me what's on your mind?"

"No, but I'm sure you're ready to listen. But tell me this bay. Why is it that whenever it looks as though there's a problem or something you don't want to deal with or that may be uncomfortable you feel that you have to run to the bottle?"

"Oh, my God. You have the problem and you're trying to make me the scapegoat. Any first year psychology student knows that's what's called misplaced aggression. Why don't you own up to the fact that whatever issue it is it's yours and stop trying to place blame. Damn! Just say what's on your mind and maybe we can come up with some sort of resolve instead of going to war when you know damn well that we don't have any animosity towards each other other than what you're trying to contrive. Hell, baby you know that I love you more than life itself and you want to argue and fight with me over something like my drinking when it doesn't affect you in the least. I drank when I met you and it didn't seem to bother you then so why the sudden concern now? What's the real issue baby and don't bring up some bullshit like my drinking. That's bullshit. What's really on your mind?"

"See that's exactly what I'm talking about bay. Soon as you have a drink you get nasty and treat me like one of your hos. You're always talking about how much you love me but if you loved me you wouldn't talk to me just like I'm just anybody or one of those other bitches you fucked and forgot. I'm your wife, the one who loves you to death and who always has your best interest at heart and you see how you treat me?" Syl said the tears streaming down her cheeks.

If there was one thing that shook Ant to his very core was to see his wife cry and for him to be the cause sobered him quickly. Getting up he walked around the oak dining table to Syl and wrapped his arm around her trembling shoulders. She shook his attempts at comforting off.

"Don't touch me. You think you can say anything and then just wrap your arms around me and that's supposed to make everything okay. I'm tired of you hurting me."

"And I'm tired of you being so damn dramatic. Ain't nobody said anything to you that should have you crying like a damn two year old that doesn't get her way."

Syl stared at him with a glare that sent daggers through him.

"You know I had reservations about saying what I've been mulling over for the past couple of months. I was trying to find a way to say it without hurting you. I don't know how many times I rehearsed what I was going to say to you so afraid what I had to say might hurt you in some way but you just don't give a damn do you when it comes to what you say or how you talk to me."

"Oh please Syl. I'm so tired of you always being so damn theatrical. If you have something to say please by all means go ahead and speak your mind."

"Fine Anthony. I was just thinking how backward we are as a race of people. We're like puppets in a puppeteer's hands with his pulling the strings governing our every move. He tells us to strive for excellence and we do that as if he holds the pot of gold at the other end of the rainbow. We go into debt to attend the best colleges and universities the nation has to offer and when we get out if we're lucky he'll throw us some kibbles and bits to keep us striving on his behalf. We work just as we did back in slavery. We run twice as fast, work twice as hard, are more driven, and more persistent than even he is and for what? And all our efforts elicit is a pat on the back. Is that how we benefit? No, we benefit by driving the same late model car and buying a house in the same neighborhood next door to him. That's how we benefit and we're so happy that he grants us these things that we forget that we're doing the labor, putting forth the effort. We are what Malcolm used to refer to as a White folks nigga or house niggas. But why Ant, please tell me why we can't ever be in the lead on anything. Why can't we be self-sufficient instead of subservient?"

"Oh okay, right. I guess I should don a sheet and walk up and down Wall Street hustlin' incense and oils. Is that your idea of self-sufficiency?" Anthony said a sarcastic smirk adorning his face.

"You know what? You're mean and ugly when you drink. You asked me what was on my mind and I try to tell you and you get nasty. I'm trying to tell you what's on my mind."

Anthony got up and tried to embrace his wife who was passionately trying to plea her case. Syl pushed him away again.

"Don't touch me."

Seeing her annoyance he backed away.

"All I'm saying is that ol' man Mitchell has been promising you a partnership in the firm for close to ten years and you're no closer to getting it than you were when you joined the firm. You'll be old and gray waiting on them to make you a partner."

"Thanks Syl. You really know how to stroke your man's ego."

"I'm just being real bay. You know that I would never say anything to hurt you but you're in denial baby. As long as you're making money for them why in the hell would he give you anything? I mean if he had any common sense he would see that giving you a part of the firm would not only assure your loyalty and your longevity with Mitchell and Ness. But when greed and racism raise their ugly head people are often blinded and lose all sight of logic. It would inevitably make more sense to make you a partner but he's so jaded by greed and his ego that he can't see a Black man in a position to usurp him and his authority that he would rather stand pat than to move ahead even if it could possibly mean millions of dollars in revenues."

"Well, I certainly can't argue with any of that. But you're preaching to the choir Syl. I think we're both conscious of that at this point."

Ignoring him she continued. He'd asked what was on her mind and she was doing just that and any sarcastic patronization wasn't going to deter her now.

"You know what they say bay. Power corrupts. Absolute power corrupts absolutely. Mitchell has been corrupted to such an extent that he can't see the demise of the empire that he built. He can't see anything but he knows that he has a goldmine in you and he thinks in meeting with you once a week he can keep tabs on how you feel and where you are. And as long as you appear content in the role that he has for you why should he shake things up. How would Bill Bixby or J.D. feel if he made you a partner? And ol' man Ness would have a coronary if he even mentioned making you a partner."

"Again you're preaching to the choir Syl. But you go ahead and vent if it makes you feel better. I look at it differently. You must think I'm more than a little naive if you think I haven't thought of all the things you're saying. I told you, you were preaching to the choir but it's more like you're just adamant about rubbing salt into an open wound."

"That wasn't my intention."

"Then please tell me what it is 'cause I'm telling you and I'm being real that I am totally lost. I've always been the sort of person that if I recognize a problem in someone else then I just do but if I don't have a solution then why bother stating the obvious because nine times out of ten if I can see the problem then chances are that the person with the problem is aware of it as well." Anthony poured himself another glass of scotch and this time fixed Syl one as well. Handing her the glass he continued. "Only the difference between you and I," he said smiling "is that I'm solution oriented and when I state the problem I've also come up with a plan, a remedy, a solution to the problem. I'm not just rubbing salt in the wound. What good does that do but cause hurt and pain just like you've done tonight and you claim you love me. For ten years I've known that I wasn't just one of the better brokers at Mitchell and Ness but was one of the better brokers on Wall Street and yet I've yet to receive my due. What!?! You don't think that shit is hard to swallow. Do you know how many of my co-workers and fellows from the other brokerages have asked me why I stay there? Do you know how many nights while you lie in the bed sleeping soundly I wrestle, tossing and turning trying to resolve myself to the fact that my life is slowly slipping by and I'm no better off than I was ten years ago when I graduated from college? Sure I make a very nice salary that many a broker would be envious of but money is by no means and end in itself. I need more. I need to see growth as a man, as a person and in my career. And I do—well I do everywhere else but my career."

"That's what I'm saying."

"I got that Syl."

"Well why don't you do something about it?"

Sipping the last sip from his glass Anthony looked at Syl in amazement.

"And what the fuck should I do about it Syl?"

"Open your own firm bay."

Anthony burst out laughing.

"I'm serious. You know the market up and down. See that's what I'm talking about. We as a people see the difficult as being impossible when in reality it's not impossible just an unforeseen challenge."

"Conceptualizing is wonderful and you're right I do know the market and its inner workings inside out but it takes more than just the knowledge to make it work. You have to have the capital just to get it off the ground and where am I going to get the startup capital and the investors to back me?"

"From everything you've told me Mitchell and Ness were just two poor white boys with an idea."

"Yeah and they were white."

"Oh hell I see how this works. Why is it that we all use color when it's convenient or when the going gets tough. Hell, we'll be Black as long as we live but does that mean we can't attain anything we set our minds to. People still are amazed that Hannibal crossed the Alps with elephants and that Egyptians built the pyramids. And before they shut it down at night did they look and say this is impossible or make excuses. They just did the damn thing. I thought my man was from the same cloth, the same ilk but instead my man who claims to be solution oriented would rather shy away from the solution than to man up and take the bull by horn and start his own firm."

"Are you quite finished," Ant said smiling.

"What the hell are you smiling about? I'm dead serious bay. Maybe I have more faith in you than you have in yourself but I know you could head Mitchell and Ness and they know that too. But they're not going to put a Black man in that position and you know it."

"You know I love you Syl. I love the fact that you believe in me and the only reason I'm smiling is because of your correlation to me and Hannibal and the great pharaohs of Egypt and their building of the pyramids. I thought I had a rather inflated sense of self-worth but it ain't got nothing compared to the pedestal you put me on," Anthony laughed eliciting a smile causing Sylvia to smile as well. "I'm sure if I hadn't interrupted you, you would have me up there with King and O'bama too," he laughed again.

"Go to hell Anthony. All I'm saying is not to limit yourself. You can do it. You don't have to be submissive to them. You can be and do whatever you want to. You're one of the brightest Black men I know and I have no idea about your expertise in trading stock. What I do know is that everyone in the business gives you a huge deal of respect based on your expertise and I know just from knowing you that anyone who garners that kind of respect from his peers is special and if you're anything close to being the man you are on the floor that you are at home then you ought not be working for anyone. They should be working for you."

"I hear you babe and I appreciate all the kudos but the reality of it all is that you have to have the capitol to embark on such a venture as opening your own firm. And the backing. I have neither."

"Then get it. Set your goals and then achieve them. I don't know how much money you need but you know how to get it."

"I do?"

"Yes you do and between the two of us we can do the damn thing bay."

Anthony chuckled.

"Between the two of us we don't have a pot to piss in or a window to throw it out of. As my father used to say we don't have enough peas together to make pea soup."

"Underestimate yourself but don't ever underestimate me Anthony Pendleton. Didn't think I was marrying a loser, a quitter. I thought I was marrying a mover; an earth shaker and I still have faith in the man I married.

I think you've been dissuaded, emasculated, put asunder and waylaid for a lack of better words which was the sole intent of Mitchell and Ness to keep you under their thumb from day one. But it's up to you to pick up the gauntlet and finish the race like you started it with all the verve and gusto of the Anthony Pendleton I saw and fell in love with."

"Wish I could babe."

"Wish you could? What the fuck is that? You can and you will. If you want me to continue to be your loving and supportive wife you will and you can best believe that."

"So what are you saying Syl?"

"Did I stutter? I said if you want me to continue to be your wife in the same capacity that I am now you're going to get up off your ass and work your ass off not to make me proud but to make yourself proud. What do you bring home bay? A few hundred thou a year—enough to make any woman happy but I'm not just any woman and when I see my husband unhappy because he's being held back from being everything he can be and his growth stunted and his masculinity undermined and demeaned I can say with no regrets to fuck the money and do you. Take a chance at being what your heart yearns for and that is to exceed even your expectations in the pursuit of self-satisfaction and happiness."

"Damn fine speech lady. I'd vote for you if I could but I believe I've already ready cast my vote and that's why I'm in the position I'm in today."

"Seriously though, Ant. I refuse to sit by idly while I watch you wither away because you're growth is being stunted by a company that gives less than a fuck about the man I love. I'd rather be broke, struggling on the come up than watch you sell yourself to the devil in an attempt to provide me with the lifestyle you figure I deserve. C'mon bay give me more credit than that. I'd leave you first rather than to see you sell your soul to the devil and Mitchell and Ness are the devil."

"And so you propose that I start my own firm. That's your solution?"

"I think it's plausible. Yes, I do. And the only thing I believe that's standing in the way is your commitment."

"That and money," Ant chuckled.

"We'll get the money bay."

Anthony laughed again.

"And how do you propose we do that. Do you know what the firm is worth? Somewhere in the neighborhood of ten or twelve million. And what do we have in the savings and checking combined? Maybe about two hundred and fifty thousand. That's a far cry from ten or twelve million."

"Both Mitchell and Ness are in their seventies and you can best believe they didn't start off with millions. And I seriously doubt if they started with a quarter of a million dollars. They started with an idea and from that they accrued their wealth. You not only have the ideas but the capitol to get started and throw in another fifty or sixty grand from your 401K and with my support there's no way you can fail."

"I hear you but we're gonna need a lot more than that."

"All things in time bay. I wanna go down and see mama for a couple of days. Maybe I can do a little fund raising while I'm there."

Anthony laughed out loud.

"My wife, my wife," he exclaimed. "I tell her I need a couple of million to start a brokerage house and she tells me that while she's going out-of-state to visit her mother she'll do a little fundraising on my behalf. Sometimes I wonder if I'm married to Sylvia Pendleton or the first lady," he laughed. "Of course if I had to make a choice I'd choose you hands down."

"Don't knock Michelle. You know Barack wouldn't be nearly as successful if it weren't for ol' girl."

"I'm sure. They say behind every good man there's a good woman."

"No doubt. Now come here honey and show you just how good I can be," Syl said pulling Anthony to her, where she kissed him deeply, passionately while unbuckling his pants and sliding them to the floor and pushing him back into the chair. Lifting her skirt to her waist she straddled the chair and found his already hard penis. She could almost see it throbbing, begging for her when she mounted him and eased down on it. Closing her eyes as she did so she rode him until she felt him spasm and erupt all in the same motion. She'd already come twice and was closing in on a third time when he came but not to be denied rode him until she felt a third one and then collapsed in closure.

"I love you Syl," he said as kissed her gently on the forehead as he lay her down in the bed. Smiling and half asleep she only faintly heard him when he asked her when she was leaving and managed to mutter.

"My flight leaves at eight thirty out of Kennedy so I have to be up by five. I already set the alarm for you for seven. I shouldn't be more than a few days. I'll call you when I get into Raleigh-Durham."

Anthony smiled.

"I know my wife and she doesn't do anything without giving it a great deal of thought so can I ask you honestly how long you've been planning this."

"Planning what? I had no idea mama was going to have a bout with her diabetes."

"I know that sweetie but everything else is preordained. Trust. I know my wife and she doesn't do anything without giving it considerable thought so if you mention a little fundraising effort it means that you've walked your way through all of this and were only keeping me –uh—shall we say informed of what was in store for me."

Syl smiled and closed her eyes before going to sleep. She was spent.

Chapter 2

The Jersey morning came in with achilly bite in the air. It was unseasonably warm considering it was March but there was still that nip in the air that made getting up just that much harder. Syl yearned for those warm North Carolina mornings and wondered briefly why she'd even considered New York. Her two previous marriages had left her more than comfortable.

She'd never mentioned her financial state to Anthony and he'd never asked. He was a traditionalist in that sense and saw it as the man's role to earn and support the wife and family. They had qualms about it at first but after a while she'd fallen into the role almost as if she were bred to be a housewife. Being a housewife from Anthony's standpoint was not what one thought of as a typical housewife. With a cook and a maid there was really little her to do other than coordinate dinner parties and decorate the rather modest home. Syl enjoyed this and after a year of feverishly decorating she'd only manage to decorate half all with Anthony's undying approval. There was only one thing that fascinated her more and that was her work with the Literacy Library, her own creation where she facilitated a tutorial program working with Harlem youth. In the three years since she'd founded it it had met with all types of accolades including New York mayor Michael Bloomberg applauding her efforts and Newark mayor and close personal friend Mayor Booker making a plea to have it added to the Newark school system as part of their after school program. Syl wondered about Mayor though. He was always a little bit more enthusiastic than what seemed necessary and everyone including mama thought that his exuberance went above and beyond the call of duty.

Syl smiled as she loaded her luggage into the car. She'd need both mayors if she were to have a chance of pulling her little coup off as well as a host of others she'd managed to stay in touch with over the years. She'd need all of them to get her plan off the floor and raise the monies to help launch the firm but as she boarded the plane and turned off the tiny cell phone she realized that if half of the ones she'd left messages for this chilly spring morning would return her calls she'd be in fine shape on her return. She never chased a dollar a day in her life but for some unknown reason she seemed to always be in the midst of the rich and the beautiful. And with her charisma and personality, accruing a couple of million was not beyond reason. And if worse came to worse she could always call on her former suitor the very unscrupulous Alexander Dumont.

The hour and forty five minute flight was smooth and without incident other than some mild turbulence and Sylvia whose fear of flying was only surpassed by her fear of rejection had taken out the tiny silver flask of Absolut and mixed it with the orange juice the petite, young stewardess brought. Now getting off the plane she wished she had withstood the turbulence. Nauseous and her lips dry she took out her lipstick and compact in an attempt to wet her dry mouth and regain her composure. Feeling a bit out of sorts, Sylvia tried to think back. Was it something she'd eaten? No, she hadn't had anything really out of the ordinary so why was she feeling so fatigued. She'd ridden Anthony like there was no tomorrow but she did that every night. Grabbing a bagel, a cup of coffee and a Wall Street Journal she headed for Budget Rent a Car.

A very nice young salesman was more than happy to wait on the stately Ms. Pendleton. Overwhelmed by her shapely legs and more than ample bust, he stared incredulously and made halfhearted attempts to flirt offering her every discount and perk he could muster. Sylvia could only smile and hoped that the rest of her meetings would have the same affect. An hour later she pulled up in front of her mother's home. She'd given her mother the house after her second husband Tristan had been killed. He'd owned a construction company and had it built for her. The house was nothing short of grand but following his death she had no use for it and it only reminded her of her late husband so she'd given it to her mother and moved back to New York. Mama was getting up in age and with diabetes and high blood pressure she made sure that she had a maid and a part time nurse who stopped in twice a week to check on her. Mama always independent fought her at every turn but being that she was taking care of Sylvia's son, Chris, now three Sylvia wouldn't be deterred. The house looked as good as it had when it had been first built and the groundskeepers were hard at work when Sylvia pulled up in front the fountain in the front yard that bubbled water and a tear came to her eyes as she remembered the day Tristan labored with her over the idea that the fountain was a bit too much. She thought it gave off the wrong impression and didn't want to give off the impression that they were some uppity Negroes. He, on the other hand, just laughed and said to hell with what people thought. He was building a castle for his princess and since he couldn't have a moat the fountain would have to do. Laughing, she conceded. Now she stood here, a tear in her eye and reflected.

They'd never caught his killer but despite that she knew who it was that had murdered Tristan and aside from liquidating his assets she'd done little in the way of revenge for her husband's murder. But now she had other plans.

Walking up the long winding driveway a myriad of thoughts ran through Sylvia's mind. Mama had insisted on Syl leaving the boy there saying that he needed a good wholesome environment to grow up in as if she couldn't provide that for her only son. Syl had conceded not because she agreed with mama but because the bond the two had was so close and mama was getting up there in age she knew that Chris' being there would infuse new life into the old woman.

She hadn't quite made it to the house when the door opened it up and Chris and mama both emerged.

"Mommy!" Chris said running out and grabbing his mother's leg. Sylvia picked the small child up and hugged him and with her free hand and then hugged her mother. She was more than glad to see them both and a deep sigh of relief came over her, the kind of relief one can only feel when they are back in the bosom of life, of home.

Once inside it was though Sylvia had never left.

"You know Ms. Johnson passed away."

"Not Lenora's mother."

"Yeah Lenora and Tee Tee's mother. Talk about a funeral. There were folks here from Louisiana and Alabama. Would have done Sarah proud if she could have seen it. She was sho loved. Them gals was to' up though. 'Specially your friend Lenora. She really broke down. They had to carry her out of there."

"Why didn't you call me mama? You know I would have come."

"I don't know. Funerals don't really affect me much. I mean it ain't no big deal. I s'spect it's because the person is already gone. The way I figures it it's what you do when a person's living that counts. When they dead it's all an afterthought. Long as that woman lived and the hard times she been through in her last days, unable to eat and provide herself and nobody there to look after her—well that's when she needed somebody. Not when they lay her to rest. If anything that's guilt. Do for people when they living then when you know you've done all you can you don't boohoo you just say she was a good woman and I did everything I could. That's why Lenora felt so bad. She ain't come down here once to see her ailin' mom and she right there in Fayetteville—not even an hour away."

"I hear you. Would never think of treating my mama that way," Syl said pulling her mother close and kissing her on the cheek.

"You had better upbringing chile. I wouldn't think no chile of mine would ever be so selfish. I'm blessed. I really am blessed to have a child like you Syl. But there is something that I wanted to talk you about and you can tell me it's none of my business if you want but don't you think that this house is a bit too much for just me and the boy. I mean ten bedrooms. Ain't but the two of us and half the time he sleeps in the bed with me. And that nurse you got and insist on me having. I'm still tryna find out what her purpose is."

Syl bowed her head and smiled. She knew mama resented the nurse but Mrs. Stansfield was more than just a nurse. She was Syl's eyes and ears. Whereas mama would never say anything to upset or raise concern Mrs. Stansfield wouldn't hesitate to call her and give her the skinny on what was really going on with mama and Chris.

"It would be one thing if she just came to check on my sugar and blood pressure. That would be one thing. But she's just too damn nosy, always prying and sticking her nose into things that don't concern her. I wouldn't be surprised if she's calling you and giving you a blow-by-blow of everything that goes on here."

Syl smiled.

"I knew it. I knew it. I knew that little snotty nosed heifer couldn't be trusted. She is reporting to you isn't she?"

"Now you're just being downright paranoid," Syl said still smiling. "You act like I've got Homeland Security watching you," she said laughing.

"I know my daughter and it may not be Homeland Security but I know you've got someone spying on me," her mother laughed. "How are you doing anyway? How are things on the home front? How's that fine young man doing and why didn't he come?"

"Anthony's fine. Working hard as usual."

"He would have to be to keep my spoiled ass daughter happy."

"I'm happy."

"But is he?"

"I suppose. He's been with the same firm for a little over ten years now and I think he's a little discouraged or disenchanted because they offered him a partnership just as a means of keeping him there but that was years ago and the way it seems now is like they aren't thinking about him."

"He's still getting paid isn't he?"

"Yes, he's being compensated nicely."

"That's the thing about these new niggras. Give them a little rope they think they a cowboy. Give them a lotta rope and they end up hangin' themselves. Tell that boy to take the money and sit tight until he finds a way to make his money work for him."

"Exactly what I told him mama. Told him to keep his mouth shut and open up his own firm."

"Only way to do it. You don't wait on nobody to give you nothing. Nobody gonna give you nothing but the good Lord and all he's gonna give you is the fortitude to go out there and get it if you really desire it."

"Oh, my God! That's the exact same thing I told him,"

"And?"

"And what? I told him to man up and if he wasn't where he wanted to be in his life and career then make it happen."

"And?"

"Told him if he wanted to keep me as his wife then to stop crying over spilt milk and do the damn thing."

"Syl!!"

"Sorry mama. It's just that Anthony has so much talent and is so good at what he does but he lets people dictate to him."

"Not with you there. If he doesn't have the backbone with you as his wife he'll learn to have some soon or get washed away with the tide. He don't know what I know. He better get some control or he'll end up broke and homeless."

Syl laughed.

"I think he'll be alright. Just needs to take my assertiveness training course."

"I'm surprised you don't already have him enrolled."

"I do. He just doesn't know it yet. Told him I was coming to see you and was going to do a little fundraising while I was here."

"And?"

"He laughed but didn't take me seriously but when I go back and put the money in front of him he'd better stand up. That'll be his wake up call. I'll see what kind of man I'm really married to. There aren't a lot of men out there that refer to themselves as successful who will let a woman outshine them or earn more than they do. The male ego can be a wonderful tool at times. And Anthony's the type that believes a woman should be at home while he provides. If I step in the house with a considerable chunk of change and I don't work and as far as he's concerned the only assets I have are him he will fall over. I'm just hoping that when he gets up he takes the gauntlet and sprints to the finish line."

"Either that or he's gonna fall over dead or hate you for being even more successful than he is with all of his expertise and no how."

"Well, I just hope it's not the latter. But I can't worry about his shortcomings now. I've got a busy week ahead of me trying to elicit some major money from the few people that I know with enough to invest."

"Who'd you have in mind?"

"You'll see," Syl said grinning widely.

"I know that look. Don't you get yourself into any trouble."

"Trouble's my middle name."

The week went fairly smoothly with her meeting with several rather prominent North Carolina businessmen and eliciting a number a number of rather positive responses. All were waiting for that one investment from someone of prominence before taking the risk of investing themselves but as resourceful as she was she was having a hard time nailing it down. And after four days she had only amassed a paltry ninety thousand dollars. Her last best hope was Newark mayor, Mayor Booker who was playing hard to get hard tutorial program in the Newark public schools. But that only amounted to a couple of hundred thousand and that was over a two-year period. And in reality that had nothing to do with the mayor but only his gift of oratory in front of the city council and getting them to buy into the program. Investing in the firm was different. She needed him to put up his own money and by doing so he could readily convince others that he believed it to be a worthwhile and potentially profitable investment.

Sylvia drove into Raleigh on Friday morning and checked into the Marriott. Mayor Booker was to arrive on a twelve o'clock and had a two hour layover on his way to Miami to meet with some businessmen he was trying to get to invest in Newark's growing infrastructure.

Sylvia checked the mini bar in the room and finding it fully stocked still felt the inclination to order a bottle of Chivas. Checking the time she noticed it was already eleven thirty. Still, the airport was nowhere and she knew that flights were almost never on time and so with reckless aplomb she grabbed a glass dropped a couple of cubes in it and poured a healthy glass of Chivas. Opening her pocketbook she grabbed a cigarette and her lighter and a small jar, which she placed on the table. After lighting the cigarette and swallowing most of the scotch in the glass she poured herself another and drank that almost as quickly as she had the first and then refilled it. The scotch had a warming sensation and she was now glad that she'd told mama that she'd probably be gone 'til tomorrow. Finishing the second glass Sylvia pulled the full-length black dress up past her more than ample chocolate mocha thighs and spread her legs widely. She had purposely not worn any panties for just this reason. Opening the jar she stuck two fingers in and rubbed her fingers together lubricating each evenly. With her free hand she spread the lips of her vagina before placing her well lubricated fingers on the tip of her clitoris. She missed Anthony's penis massaging her clit. It had been a day since she'd felt his penetrating jabs and though this was hardly a replacement it would have to suffice at least for now. She was tight but with each gentle caressing massage she could feel herself becoming more wet until she fell in rhythm with the motion.

"Ummm," Syl moaned as she let her head fall back and raised her leg to the table. Massaging slowly in tiny circles she began to feel her heartbeat quicken as her breasts rose and fell with each thrust. Afraid of coming to soon she lessened the pressure and felt herself falling and then just as quickly as she fell she rose again and this time there was no stopping her as she arched her ass up off the chair and applied more pressure to her clit. She was coming now with each stroke and as she did she groaned and cursed almost as if she were exorcising some demon from her body. Spent and exhausted Sylvia stood smoothed her dress, redid her makeup and staggered briefly before regaining her composure and heading to the door. Minutes later she entered Raleigh Durham International Airport.

"Gate 16", she muttered to herself. Though never one for flying Sylvia loved the feeling she got from airports with the constant rush of travelers heading here and there trying to catch departing planes. She liked to imagine the people traveling to exotic places and the feeling of loved ones anxiously awaiting always gave her a warm feeling. And although she liked and admired Mayor Booker she was not altogether happy with the task at hand or the probabilities. Nevertheless she had a job to do and if she did it well it would help her husband whom she loved deeply leapfrog from the muck and the mire to the position in life he so richly deserved and despite the denials wrought from the very root of racism he would now achieve.

"Mayor Booker," Syl said smiling as she noticed the distinguished young man sitting reading a Raleigh tabloid.

"Sylvia," he said grabbing her and hugging her before pushing her away to take a good long look at the woman in front of him. "Goodness gracious! Is it me or do you get better looking every time I see you?"

"Oh mayor you're a middle age woman's dream with all your flattery. No wonder you went into politics," she laughed. "You certainly know the right thing to tell your constituents. I'm not a resident of Newark but if I were you'd certainly get my vote. Have you been waiting long?"

"Thought I was until I saw you. The wait was damn well worth it now that I see you."

"Oh mayor. Stop it. Thank goodness I'm dark-skinned or you'd see me blushing."

"Come now Sylvia you can't tell me that I'm the first person that has commented on your charm and beauty. I'm sure I'm not even the first person today."

"Actually you are," she laughed. "When you get to be my age the wolf whistles and cat calls turn into shrieks of horrors."

"Don't know what their seeing but I'm seeing the same thing that dynamo of a husband of yours saw. I'm still trying to understand how he pulled off that coup. Snatched you right from under my watchful eye. Me— well I've always been a little too slow when it came to seizing the opportunity. I was giving you time to grieve after Tristan was killed and the next thing I knew I was looking at your picture of you in the New York Post's gossip pages standing next to Anthony with a caption stating that you were engaged to be married. I was crushed. I had all intentions of being next in line so the news hit me like a sledgehammer. I mean I was floored."

"Oh please mayor. You crushed? I saw you on CNN a couple of months ago and I think it was Piers Morgan that was interviewing you and he was talking about the transformation of the city and he made a reference to Newark taking on the personality of its mayor and then there was a speech you gave. I do believe it went a little something like this. 'We're Brick City because we're tough, we're resilient, we're strong, we're enduring and, most important, when we come together there's nothing we can't create.' I do believe those were your words."

The mayor laughed.

"You saw that huh? And not only did you see it you got me down verbatim."

"Some things tend to stick with me especially if they're refreshingly relevant."

"And that was?"

"To me it was because I saw Newark some years ago when Gibson and James had it and although they put forth a good effort the transformation under your tenure has been remarkable. A lot of people have you as the natural successor to Barack."

The mayor laughed heartily.

"Okay sister. I know you have an agenda but don't you think you're laying it on a little thick now?"

"I'm sure a man in your position is astutely aware of not only his detractors but also those columnists in his corner and you know as well as I do that there have been many comparisons drawn between you and O'bama."

"I've heard a few comparisons and and am an optimist but the comparisons to Barack and I are certainly premature and highly unlikely. Look at what Barack has done and the amount of time he did it in. In 2000 he was almost an unknown entity. His meteoric rise is nothing but sheer genius and then in an election that he went into as the underdog he galvanized the young people and virtually ran away with the victory. I haven't done anything remotely comparable. Here I am sitting in Raleigh Durham International Airport and there is little or no recognition."

"Right now," Syl retorted.

"Right now what?"

"Right now there may be little or no recognition but that's only a temporary situation as I'm sure you know. In a couple of years after you secure the political machine to launch you into the national spotlight you know it's a wash. I've watched you come of age since you became mayor in '06 and you're every bit the speaker Barack is and you certainly have the fire and desire so for you it's just a matter of time. Am I lying?"

The mayor always the politician smiled but did not consent.

"May I ask where we're going?"

"I have a suite at the Marriot. Thought maybe we could discuss a proposal I'd like to put forth for you. When's your meeting in Miami?"

"Not 'til tomorrow afternoon. I came a day early so I could bask in that Miami sun for a day or so. I love Newark but the weather can be brutal this time of year."

"Who you telling? North Carolina's my home and as much as I love the city and all of its culture I try to come home as much as possible during the cold months. It ain't nothing pretty about Jersey and New York this time of year."

At the door to her suite Sylvia fished through her pocketbook for her card. Finding it she realized that as resigned to making a proposal that he couldn't refuse she was still somewhat nervous about the whole affair.

"Hungry," she asked.

"A little but not necessary for the edible kind but we can talk about that after I hear what you have in store for me," he said smiling sheepishly.

"Mayor."

"I think if it's alright that I call you Sylvia it would be appropriate if you called me Mayor."

"Okay Mayor. Would you like a drink?"

"Chivas is it?"

"You have a good memory. Chivas it is."

"That's fine but remember I'm not much of a drinker. Two fingers should do me fine."

"On the rocks or straight up?"

"A little ice would be fine."

Taking the glass Sylvia turned to go to the refrigerator only to hear the mayor gesture approvingly as she walked away. Moments later she was back. Handing the glass to the mayor she opted for ginger ale still feeling the liquor she had prior to picking the mayor up. Not sure another glass wouldn't hinder her presentation she deferred. She watched him as he sipped from the glass and when most was gone picked up his glass and headed back to the fridge. Handing him the glass he smiled, lust overcoming the glaze from the liquor. Noticing it she asked. "Is everything okay Mayor?"

"Couldn't be better. You know it's so seldom I get to kick back and just relax. Feels good. But enough about me. What's on the table?"

"Actually I have a proposal for you that involves quite a large sum of money."

"Is there a proposal that doesn't?"

"No, I suppose there isn't. Only this one doesn't involve the city per se. It's a proposal concerning Black folks and their lack of recognition in this country. As you know most of the money is tied up with the top one percent and that one per cent just happens to be Caucasian. There is an eroding middle class and an ever-expanding poverty level. Outside of a few Blacks like yourself we control nothing," pausing she smiled. "Anthony would say I'm preaching to the choir so let me get down to the essence of my proposal. When Bin Laden attacked the World Trade Center with the idea of crippling America and bringing her to her knees he went for the countries financial capitol. It is as it was a hundred years ago still Wall Street and it is as it was a hundred years ago still a bastion of White America. Now I'm sure you've been keeping abreast of my husband's meteoric rise to fame and acclaim in the financial journals and I don't know if you realize how he's taken the firm of Mitchell and Ness from an average brokerage to one of the elite brokerage firms on Wall Street. In his tenure with Mitchell and Ness they have grown a little over two hundred percentage points and each growth spurt can be readily attributed to his bringing in another client and successfully managing their monies. Here's the correlation between the companies growth and his acquisitions and as you can see there is a direct correlation. Anthony has personally accounted for a little over sixty million dollars since he's been with the firm."

"And I'm sure Mitchell and Ness has compensated his hard work and perseverance in kind."

"That they have," Syl said careful not to bite the hand that was feeding her. "But Anthony and I came to the conclusion after several years of mulling this over. Sure we are comfortable but isn't it time mayor that we're represented among the folks that shape this country. The real earth shakers in our capitalistic system are the ones with the capitol. And it's high time we started bartering on our own behalf. It's high time we started affecting some change from a position of power. And so what we are suggesting is the first Black owned brokerage firm on Wall Street headed up by none other than 2006's Wall Street Man of the Year, Anthony Pendleton. All we need is the startup capital but more than that we need well-known name and hot commodity to invest in us so that other wealthy yet less known men of prominence will come get on board. I met with the board of trustees for Mutual Life—you known the first and now the largest Black owned insurance company in the country. Met with them yesterday and they're mulling over the proposal but they're like everyone else. They're looking to see who's going to come forward and make the first move. If you could come forward and make that pledge Mayor it will be like a stampede, like the Forty-Niners gold rush. You're the face we need to head the campaign. Do you think there's even a remote possibility that you might be able to be that face?"

"What kind of money are we talking?"

"Well, in all sincerity we're looking for at least half a mil."

"Whoa! Hold up baby girl. I'm the mayor of Newark. I don't own it. Five hundred thousand dollars is a lot of money. The best I could probably do is a hundred and twenty five—maybe a hundred and fifty."

Sylvia's smile spread across her face knowing that his endorsement meant more than any dollar amount he could give her. Still, she never said a word and was content to let his attorney and accountant check it out. The mayor was on his third drink and his eyelids were unusually droopy.

"You okay Mayor?"

"I'm fine. I told you I'm no drinker," he said almost apologetically. "Just need to lie down for a few."

"You do that. Do you need some help to the bedroom?"

"No I'm good,' he said staggering and doing everything not to fall on his way to the bed.

Syl smiled. The scag she dumped in his drink was having just the effect it should have had.

"You need anything Mayor?" Syl asked attempting to sound concerned.

"Nothing but you precious."

"Give me a minute and I'll be right there," she lied.

And as if on cue there was a faint knock at the door and two busty young ladies entered.

"He's in the bedroom," Syl said handing each girl a Benjamin.

"I want you ladies to work him over real good while we make this little movie of the mayor with not one but two high class call girls.

"Oh my God you're not going to black mail him are you? Because if you are I don't want any parts of this."

"No, this is just a little insurance so he doesn't renig on our little business deal. If he holds to his part of the deal chances are he'll never know a movie was made. But what I need for you girls to do is to work him over real well from head to toe. I want him moanin' in the morning and doing his rendition of Frankie Beverly's Joy and Pain, understand?"

"Gotcha, Ms. Pendleton. The same as that trustee member from Mutual of Life?"

"Yes ma'm. The very same way."

The mayor was sound asleep by the time Syl and the two call girls entered the bedroom and Syl who had never been in the least bit attracted to women even when her sorors in college had been dabbling in same gender sex had to admit that the tall leggy brunette with the thirty eight double D's was quite attractive. The other a comely short blonde was no slouch either and Syl thought them a steal for a hundred apiece. The women knew their trade too and as the tall brunette with the Ecstasy tattoo on her upper thigh undressed the mayor and turned him on his back the tiny blonde climbed on top putting her pussy in his face and rode him with all the gusto of a jockey at the Belmont Sweepstakes while the tall brunette sucked the mayor's penis 'til it stood on its own and throbbed to reach her juicy red lips. Syl stood there camcorder in one hand and felt her own libido rise as she filmed and watched the two women make love. They did everything short of making the mayor come and when Syl said that's enough she was surprised when the tall brunette stopped sucking on the mayor's penis and stood up only to stand up and pull him to the edge of the bed before climbing on top and riding him until she threw her head back and screamed in ecstasy.

"Damn that was good," she said as she wiped herself off, a grin as wide as the moon on her face.

"Wasn't it? And just imagine if he'd been awake," the short blonde added.

The two thanked Syl, dressed and exited the hotel quickly.

Syl in disbelief or rather in awe was visibly shaken and as wet as the two women that had performed the actual act. She had actually considered performing the whole thing herself but her allegiance to Anthony and their marriage wouldn't allow her to do it but now standing their watching the women and the enjoyment they seem to be having aroused her and after all she was human. The mayor was still half hard when she looked at him and with a little prodding she was sure she could have him rigid and hard again and so with the Vaseline she'd gotten out of her overnight bag she began to massage him gently, careful not to awaken him from his drug induced sleep. When he responded she pulled up the long black dress and inserted his rock hard dick into her and rode him slowly letting her pussy feel every inch of his solid member.

Exhausted and spent she got up showered and fixed herself another drink before donning a sheer white night gown and heading to the extra bedroom. Before leaving she undressed the mayor and found a pair of his pajamas in his suitcase washed him off and dressed him for bed. She then checked his ticket and found his flight for the following day departed at ten and called the front desk to leave a wakeup call for him.

Sylvia felt no remorse as she poured herself another glass of Chivas and had to admit she wanted no harm to come to the mayor as she considered him a friend but she had high expectations for the man she called her husband and would go to the ends of the earth to see that he reach and become all that he aspired to be even if it meant her selling her soul to the devil to achieve it.

The next morning Sylvia could hear the phone and listened closely to see if the mayor answered. When he did she knew he was all right and turned over and closed her eyes feigning sleep. A minute or so later she heard her bedroom door crack and the mayor calling her name.

"Yes Mayor," she said opening one eye and yawing loudly.

"Morning Syl. Goodness. That must have been some night. Feel like I was hit by a train. My whole body aches."

"You were pretty nice last night mayor." Sylvia said smiling.

"Hope I didn't do anything or saying anything inappropriate. Told you I wasn't much of a drinker."

"Not to worry. You are and have always have been the consummate gentleman much to my chagrin," Sylvia smiled.

"And what's that supposed to mean?"

"Oh, there was a time when I had a bit of a crush on you after Tristan's death but you neither seemed to notice or to care."

"Another golden opportunity missed. One of the reasons for making sure I have a capable staff. If I didn't there's no telling where I'd be," he laughed.

"And who put me to bed?"

"I took the liberty. Your suits downstairs being dry cleaned. Actually it should have been up by now. What time is it anyway?"

"Almost seven thirty."

"Okay. It should arrive along with your breakfast by eight. And I saw that your plane leaves at ten which gives you ample time."

"Sylvia you're a doll," he said leaning over the bed and giving her a sisterly peck on the cheek.

She smiled but inwardly she felt the zing from a man she had had and still desired.

"Not a problem. Anything for our next Black president."

He laughed deeply, heartily.

"With you in my corner the presidency would be a cinch."

"I'm your number one supporter. You know we Black folks gotta stick together."

"Wish you could get Richard Steele to understand that."

"Some people are unreachable. When you talk about people like that I become a firm supporter of euthanasia and abortion."

The mayor chuckled.

"Woman, you are really something. I bet you're a handful. Only regret is I may never have the opportunity to find out," he said half-heartedly although there was a good bit of sincerity in his words.

My thoughts exactly Sylvia thought, half smiling, although I do know you are all the man I imagined you would be even in your sleep.

"Friends like you are few and far between," the mayor said. "And I will have my lawyers look into your proposal and get back to you in the next few days. If everything works out you should have a check in the mail in the next few days. And after I launch the city's proposal I'll mention you to the businessmen I'm meeting in Florida later today. They're some pretty prominent brothas and always interested in a worthwhile investment. I'll telephone you and let you know how it goes. In the meantime you be good and give my regards to Anthony."

"I will do that and I thank you for taking the time Mayor. Now you hurry so I'm not the cause of you missing your flight. Now go get dressed while I go get my pretty on."

"Well that shouldn't take you long beautiful. Would be hard for you to get even more attractive."

"Thanks for the compliment. You definitely have my vote now."

The two laughed and then hugged briefly as they parted ways in the hotel lobby. Reporters who only a day earlier hadn't recognized the mayor now swarmed the hotel lobby as if there were a celebrity in their midst and I guess he was a celebrity of sorts and it was obvious that Sylvia wasn't the only one that thought Mayor Booker was on the rise."

On the road back to Elizabethtown Sylvia had a lot to think about. She was almost two hundred thousand dollars richer than when she'd arrived a week ago but she was still a mighty long ways from where she needed to be. Still, she wasn't discouraged. She knew it was entirely possible to put her hands on the money she needed but it would not only take cunning, time and when necessary some rather immoral methods. And at times like now she had to ask herself how she'd come to stray so far from the morally principled person her parents had raised her to be. Truth be known she had learned to play hardball in the world from men who took no prisoners when it came to money and the acquisition of power. From William to Alexander Dumas she had learned the politics of power and the means of obtaining it. The lessons though often more painful than she would like to recollect were still a learning process and she had learned well. They were not gender biased and if one had the resources to engage and was savvy and smart they could participate and thrive or be the latest victim of vodka and Valium. Sylvia had no intentions of doing the latter and though she was no real fan of the game she knew the rules and used her gender as part of her strategy. The seemingly very astute Mayor Booker was simply her latest pawn in this latest game of virtual chess. Still, there were bigger game out there that could bring more in the means of capital and right now capital is what she needed most.

Her first husband, William Stanton, her next logical choice would be easy. He perhaps knew her better than anyone aside from mama and was one of the few people she trusted. He'd remarried not long after their divorce and was in charge of his own firm in Charlotte and had only in the past couple of years broken into the Forbes 500. Still, he was quiet and unassuming as the day they'd met and seemed more suited to the quiet, laid back lifestyle of a Charlotte, North Carolina than the hustle and bustle of the big city. It was not uncommon for him to send her a check in the amount of fifty thousand once or twice a year just because or when he had something on his mind. Upon reception she'd always call to thank him and he'd unload just as he'd do when they were married sometimes talking until the wee hours of the morning about whatever was on his mind at that particular time. Most of the time she didn't know the intricacies or the business side of the matter but she did know people and could size up a delicate situation and proceed to advise him on the means to best handle the situation at hand. Surrounding himself with the best and brightest business and legal minds he still came to her when the chips were down. She might not know the intricacies of trading but she did know people and could read them as well as anyone and William knew and valued this attribute in his ex-wife. And Syl was there and available for him but she wondered why William would marry a woman that could not aid him in every facet of his life and career but then she knew William, so old fashioned and traditional that barefoot and pregnant was all he required—a trophy wife was really all he really desired and though he referred to her on a regular basis she may have been too high maintenance for a man with such traditional values. Still, he valued her knowledge and expertise and she his and she knew that if she was persistent in her proposal he would buy into it. Taking out her cell she phoned him directly and was surprised that he picked up on the second ring.

"William."

"Hey Syl. Well, this is a surprise. What's up beautiful? How are you love?"

"I'm good. Listen I'm down here visiting mama and I was wondering if you had any free time this afternoon?"

"Well I've got a meeting with the board of trustees at twelve but that shouldn't last too long. I should be free by one, one thirty at the latest. Why what's up?"

"Wanted to meet with you. Have a proposal I think you may be interested in."

"I'm not sure I like the sound of that. The last proposal between us wound up in divorce court and cost me more than I'd care to remember."

Sylvia laughed.

"I think you may like this proposition a lot more than the previous one. But anyway can we meet say around three in Winston-Salem or Greensboro?"

"Sounds like a plan I'll call when I get close."

"I'll do that. I'm heading that way as we speak. Guess I'll do a little shopping in St. Paul's in the meantime."

"You haven't changed much have you?"

"No, but I think you have. You've grown a lot since we were together. You don't seem to be nearly as high strung or driven."

"It's called age but Lord knows I'm really skeptical about this meeting now. You're not one to flatter. This must really mean a lot to you."

"It does and stop thinking you know me so well. I've always been straight with you William and it's not flattery. If you had been a little more laid back and a little more accommodating back then chances are we'd still be married but that's ancient history. It is what it is."

"I really think it was a little more than that but like you said it is what it is. Why don't we meet at Vito's at three? That way you can go to St. Pauls and we can grab some Italian, get a couple of carafes of wine and make an evening of it."

"I'll see you at three then."

Everything was going according to plan and she knew William was an easy touch and would give her anything she wanted. Whether it was out of guilt that their marriage had failed or the fact that he had never stopped loving her the fact remained that she had him on retainer and had every intention of letting him remain in that position. William never seemed to mind paying her alimony and continued to pay despite her marriage to Tristan and Anthony. In his mind, she would always remain to some degree his wife despite being married to Melinda.

Sylvia parked in front of the modest consignment shop in St. Paul's and was happily surprised that their inventory had been almost entirely overhauled. The owner Mrs. Wyatt, an older White woman was in attendance and greeted her warmly. She liked Sylvia knowing that Syl unlike many of her customers appreciated the finer things in life, her clothes being one of them. And Sylvia liked the old White woman and her taste in clothes. The sales people following their bosses lead showered over her leaving the other patrons virtually unattended offering her espresso and Danishes and fawning over pocketbooks and accessories they could only dream of buying as Sylvia tried any and everything on. The store carried nothing that could be considered trendy or modish as Mrs. Wyatt made it a point to specialize in fashionable but subtle elegance. Over the years the Sylvia and the older White woman had become quite close with Mrs. Wyatt often putting aside clothes for times just as this when she knew Syl would be in and today was just one of those days. The spring collection was in and the winter selection had been marked down to half price. Sylvia was in her element. Moving between the rows of clothes she fingered everything in her size but was particularly attracted to a black, full length, strapless dress with the back out that had sensual written into its very fabric. That wasn't the only thing she came across and when the two women hugged and parted ways Syl had spent close to twenty three hundred dollars and was for the most part set for the spring, summer and next winter.

Greensboro was close to two hours away and it was already one thirty but she didn't mind making William wait. As sexy as she looked it would be well worth his wait she thought and smiled to herself as she turned up the smooth jazz sounds of Rick Braun and then the pint of Hennessey. In an hour she was feeling no pain, no remorse and decided to call Anthony to see how he was faring on his end.

"How's my baby?"

"Hey Syl! Where've you been? I've been trying to reach you for the past two days. I even called your mother. You had me worried."

"Sorry baby. I was in a meeting and turned my phone on vibrate. I must have forgotten to turn it back on. I'm sorry but you know your Syl's a big girl. No need to ever worry," she laughed.

"Easy for you to say but I don't know what I'd do if something were to happento my baby. So what's good?"

"Nothing really. Everything's fine here and you?"

"Same ol'. Same ol'. Work and home. Maintainin' as best I can without my baby," he lied.

"I hope you're doing better than just maintainin'. I'm hoping you're makin' moves in my absence and trying to get this money together. I so want you to be happy and satisfied. That's one of the reasons I'm in North Carolina. I hope I'm not here busting my ass on your account while you're sitting there sipping with your legs up."

If Sylvia could have only known how close to the truth she was. A glass of patron in one hand Anthony sat in a suite at the Ritz Carlton one leg draped over the Queen Anne chair a finger to his lips to make sure his pretty blonde secretary didn't make a sound as she licked and sucked him greedily.

"I told you these things take time. Much as I want to not even I know how to go out and turn a dime into fifteen cents let alone a couple of hundred thou into the millions needed as startup costs. Be serious. Oh!" he shouted as she bit lightly on his balls summoning him in earnest now to get off the phone.

"What's wrong bay? Are you okay?" Syl said alarmed.

"Just spilt my drink on myself is all."

"Oh don't scare me like that. I thought something had happened."

"I'm a big boy too you know. But listen Syl I'm right in the middle of something so let me finish and I'll call you before I call it a night. Okay baby?"

"You haven't told me you love me."

Ant looked down at the woman between his legs.

"I'll tell you tonight sweetness. You be safe."

"And you behave yourself."

Anthony flipped the phone shut and leaned back. He was on the verge of coming but felt no emotion towards the beautiful woman who had waited so long for this opportunity to try and make an impression, to fill his needs, to somehow make him apart of her life.

"She wanted you to tell her that you loved her didn't she? You don't have to lie to me Anthony. What else would an adoring wife want than to be assured that her husband loves her? And especially one that's married to you. I can't blame her in the least. Look at me— down on my knees trying to share any part of you that I can have knowing full well that you are a happily married man."

"If I'm so happily married," Anthony said half yelling, "then why the hell am I here with my secretary?"

"I'm sorry Mr. Pendleton," the pretty young blonde said as tears ran down from her eyes.

Anthony stood and gathered himself before hugging the young woman.

"I'm sorry Samantha. It's not your fault."

"Yes, it is. I've done everything in my power to seduce you for as long as I can remember. Here me at twenty-eight walking around with some little schoolgirl crush on the teacher. I knew you were married and don't know why I had this crazy ass notion that because I was a blue-eyed, blonde girl with a tight ass you were going to leave someone as bright and beautiful as that ebony princess you go home to every night. I don't know why I even thought that. I guess I was just playing with myself. I guess I was in some kind of fantasy world and didn't want to deal with the reality of the situation."

"Don't blame yourself. I could have easily said no."

"And you did so many times that I would need a calculator to keep track but I've always been a firm believer in persistence overcoming resistance. And eventually you wore down but at no time should you think that this is your fault. I just wanted to see what it was like to be held and loved by a real man."

"And did you get a chance to live out your fantasy?"

"Well I thought I would 'til Mrs. Pendleton called."

"Well let's not let that stop what started off as a beautiful evening," he said pulling her closely to him and kissing her deeply. "I think I'm as curious to know about Ms. Samantha King as she is to know about me."

"Really?"

"Then it's not just about sex?"

"How long have we've worked together, been in the same office together, gone to lunch together?"

"Seems like forever and then again only a day."

Her baby blue eyes had always sent quivers through him. He'd grown accustomed to her voluptuous assets like her long shapely legs, her tiny waist and large protruding breasts that made many Fed Ex and UPS man do a double take. But those eyes he'd never gotten used to. And now here she was staring at him deeply exacting his feelings towards her and he was weak. Handing her a glass of wine he grabbed her by the hand and led her to canopied bed where she suddenly pulled away.

"Is this just about sex Mr. Pendleton?" She asked.

"We've laughed and joked and conversated for the last six years Samantha. Tonight it's about sex."

The young woman laughed.

"Thank you for your honesty and I'm okay with that but when you finish I want you to love me. I want a man to love me not for what I have between my legs but love me for who I am. And if you can't then just hold me and pretend that you love me. Can you at least do that for me? All I'm asking is that you return some of what I feel for you."

"And what is that?"

"Oh don't play dumb with me Mr. Pendleton."

"Call me Anthony."

"Okay Anthony. But you must know that I've loved you from the first day I came to work for you."

"Call me stupid, Samantha but I wasn't aware."

"Have you ever had a more proficient secretary?"

"Now that you mention it I don't think so."

"And you won't. If you hadn't noticed I pride myself on having things done before Mr. Pendleton asks and I pride myself on having them done not only to the best of my ability but better than he expects. It's my only way of expressing my dedication and devotion to not only my work but to the man I love as well."

"And your being here this evening is a testimony to what. It's certainly not the job."

"My job ended at two thirty today. The only job I have now is ingratiating myself with this fine Black man in front of me and although I know he may be in the love with the queen now I want to let him know that there is a princess waiting in line."

And with that Samantha undid her belt and let her pants drop to the floor revealing the black g-string in direct contrast to her smooth olive skin. Kicking her pants in front of her she turned and bent over to pick them up as to show Anthony the beautifully rounded ass he'd envisioned in his mind more times than he cared to remember. Bending over she pulled off the black turtleneck and unfastened her bra letting her dark brown nipples graze the floor. Anthony looked and found that his penis had suddenly grown hard and was throbbing even more so than before. He had always desired Samantha but over the years had gradually grown used to her being around like just another office fixture. But now she was more than just a fixture. She was real, attainable and in the flesh. Slowly she stood and turned to face him.

"Syl is one beautiful woman but does she bring all this to the table? And if she does let me ask you this can she, or better yet after I don't know how many years of marriage can she work like I'm about to? I ain't gonna lie to you Anthony. My goal is to make your love for your wife a distant memory."

"Go for it baby," was all Anthony could muster and Samantha intent on making Anthony hers did just that.

"Is it true what they say about a man wanting a lady in the living room and a ho in the bedroom."

Anthony chuckled. It was funny but he knew it was true. He was testimony to that.

"I guess to an extent it is," he chuckled.

"So, let me show you what I can bring to the bedroom," Samantha said as she pulled the covers back and beckoned for Anthony to join her. Samantha laid there her bronze body bathing beautiful against the backdrop of the white canopy almost reminding him of something from a myth lying there like a Greek goddess.

Anthony undressed quickly. Samantha was on him within seconds. Mounting him and trying to take him it was obvious that it had been sometime since she'd been with a man but if hunger and desire was a necessary prerequisite she had both and it wasn't long before she had all of him deep within her. Her blonde hair hung in his face and she said everything that she'd been thinking for the past six or seven years which did nothing but arouse Anthony to a passion he hadn't known in years.

"Damn Anthony! You don't know how many days, how many nights I've dreamed of this day. And I always knew you would be better than any man I'd ever been with or any man I would ever be with," she said as she stroked him back and forth applying little or no pressure to his penis though her small pussy gripped it tightly. Still, the sensual young blonde had no intentions of making him come. What she wanted was for him to feel her. She wanted him to know her feelings for him had nothing to do with her having an orgasm or sleeping with him but only had to do with feelings, her innermost desires and covert feelings which she had held at bay for close to seven years.

Yes, she loved him and would do whatever it was he desired to let him know. And yes she knew her chances lay somewhere between slim and none but she had to try. Even if her attempts fell short she would know she had given it her all and would have come to know the man she loved and had loved for what seemed an eternity.

Slowly, passionately she rode him until he began to groan under the relentless pressure of her riding him.

"Samantha please," was all he managed to say but she had already gotten up and grabbing the hand towel at the bottom of the bed began wiping her forehead.

"Be right back Anthony," she said wondering if her attempts at loving this chocolate piece of perfection were really having the desired effect. Still, she reckoned if they weren't they would be before the evening was over. He'd been ready, been on the verge but she'd only just begun. Returning from the bathroom where she carefully contemplated her next move Samantha bent and kissed him deeply, passionately before mounting him again—only this time with her ass in his face. Grabbing his ankles she slammed herself down on his half hard dick until it was again hard and penetrating. She was riding him now and his groans soft and subtle before were louder now and she had everything she could do now to hold on and not come. When she felt his arch back and him about to come she slid off and rolled over in a mass of wetness.

"Baby please," Anthony muttered.

"Baby please what," Samantha smiled. "What are you saying Anthony? Are you telling me that my pretty ass is something that you want or that Samantha's tight little pussy feels good to you daddy?"

"Yes," was all that Anthony could seem to get out.

"I hear you but you're gonna have to do a lot better than that to get the freak to come out in Sammy. I thought you told me that every man wants a freak in the bedroom?"

"I did."

"Then make me wanna do you baby. Make me wanna do you where I have you dreamin' wide awake. I want to make you think of me when you're in one of boring meetings you detest so. I want to make you think of me when you're wife thinks she's putting it down. I've got that kind of love and I only have that kind of love for one man. And that man is you Anthony but you have got to make me believe you want it."

"I want it baby. Trust me Samantha I want your love."

The stately young blonde smiled knowing she had him, lit a cigarette and blew the smoke out slowly.

"Are you sure you want me?"

"Yes, Sammy. I want you."

"How much?" She was toying with him now. She was a in a good place. She'd taken the man she wanted and desired and let him know that she was capable. She'd corralled him, caressed and cajoled him into thinking she controlled his fate at least on this evening but she still had her doubts.

"Do you really want me or do you just want me to make you come?"

"No, Sammy I really do want you."

"But wasn't that your wife on the phone just a little while ago? What kind of marriage is that that after ten or eleven years that you can just throw it all away for a pretty ass and a good screw? Please tell me it means more than that. Tell me it's more important than that."

Anthony could feel the rage coming to the forefront.

"What the fuck is it to you and why would you bring some shit up like that at a time like this?"

"I'm bringing it up because your wife has invested ten long years into your ass and if you can throw it all away in a night what's to say that you can't and won't do the same thing to me?"

"I very well may and can," Anthony said regaining his composure.

"Difference is I wouldn't let you. I wouldn't be working hard to keep you. You'd be begging to keep me. I know somewhere down the road you've heard the old saying that 'self-preservation is the first law of nature'. And you'd want me just as much if not more than I'd ever want you. See what Sylvia doesn't realize and most women don't is that you never love anyone more than you love yourself. And when you really love and care about yourself your partner will realize that and won't get jealous of any outside force but will be jealous of the love you have for yourself. When that becomes his or her competition they will try and exhibit more love for you than you have for yourself. It's a hard thing to accomplish but they will cherish you knowing just how much you love and care about yourself."

"You have this pretty much all thought out don't you."

"Pretty much. I mean it's not an exact science but close enough."

"Let me give you a prime example. Get up and come over here and kneel at the edge of the bed."

Anthony did as he was instructed. Samantha slid to the edge of the bed and sat up letting her legs hit the floor.

"Come here Anthony. Between my legs."

Anthony did as he was told sliding in between her legs until his eyes were eye level with her vagina.

"Now eat me Anthony. Slowly at first."

Doing as he was told Sammy grabbed the back of his head and pulled him close enough where his head filled her crotch.

"Softly Anthony. Stop acting like this is the last supper. Softly, gently baby. Mommy'll give you some more if you work it just right. That's it baby, Now put your fingers inside me baby. Easy baby. Stroke it easy baby. That's it baby. Now suck on it baby. Gently sweetie. Don't be so rough. Ooh yeah! That's it baby. Let me hear you suck on it baby. Come on sweetie let me hear you slurp on it. Ooh yeah that's good baby. Now put a finger up my ass and make me come hard baby."

Doing as he was told Anthony slid a finger up her pretty ass and watched as she began to contract around his finger her body rigid. Screaming his name loudly she came hard as he eased it out.

"Ooh yeah baby. Oh my God. That was delicious. Ooh baby." Samantha said shuddering with the aftershock. "Lord knows it doesn't take me long to come. Give me a minute Anthony and then I want you to take me there again. Only this time you know what turns me on so I won't have to say anything and I can focus. You okay with that?"

Anthony nodded. Not in a million years would she have imagined that she would be directing Anthony

Pendleton on how to make her come. She who had been following his orders and directives for as long as she could remember was now the one in charge.

"Damn that was good. I think I'm gonna need you to revisit that sweetheart but before you do let me take care of you so you're satisfied. Stand up."

Anthony stood up his dick protruding and throbbing with desire.

"Now tell me you want me baby."

"You just don't know how much."

"You'd be surprised at what I know. I know that you prefer my black pants suit to most of what I wear. I know that you like me in cowl necks that reveal the twins and you love it when I bend over your desk, my cleavage showing, and you can get a full glimpse of my breasts. You wonder whether my nipples are pink or dark brown. And you wonder how tight my ass is and if it's ever been penetrated. You wonder if I in all my correctness I'm just some goody two shoes or if I'm conscience of how truly blessed I am and can I work this body the way it should be worked. I know you like me in heels—the higher the better 'cause it gives my ass and legs more definition. How am I doing?"

"You're quite perceptive Sammy. You could sense all of this and never let on that you knew."

"That's my bread and butter Ant but it's also my job to go after the things I want or leave myself open to regrets for not putting forth the effort to acquire what I truly want in life. And so I studied you and your reactions to different things and tried to acquiesce to the things I noticed that you responded to."

Anthony could do little more than smile. He remembered telling his nephew not more than a week ago when the subject of women came up that to study a woman is like study a black widow spider. He could recall the analogy as if it were yesterday.

'Just remember this Isaiah. It's not the size of the dog but the fight in the dog. A woman is similar. Men have the physical prowess but can never defeat a woman because a woman has something that a man does not have by his very nature. A woman has the cunning and intellect to assess a situation similar to a black widow spider. A black widow spider can lure prey three to four times her size into her web and defeat them without so much as having to touch them. A woman with guile and cunning can do the same to most men luring them in and making short work of them."

"Where are you Anthony? It seems like you left me there for a minute."

Anthony's gaze felt Samantha's blonde pubic hair.

"I was just thinking about something I told my nephew."

"And I was thinking that you should follow your emotions and relax for a minute. Think later. Fuck me now," she said grabbing the back of her knees and lifting her legs 'til her feet touched her ears reveal the pink of her pussy. Always the professional and with sexual harassment suits running wild Anthony had never considered propositioning Samantha. She, on the other hand, had a different agenda and it was well in effect.

"Fuck me dammit. Stick that big, black dick in me and fuck me 'til it hurts. I want this shit to be sore.

Every time I take a step I want to remember Anthony Pendleton's dick up in me. Now fuck me Anthony."

Folding her legs in front of her face only opened her pussy wider and gave Anthony a clear view of the tunnel he was about to enter. Spitting on his throbbing dick he slid it in as far as it would go.

Samantha screamed.

"Oh my God! Easy big boy!"

"Thought you said you wanted me to tear the shit up. Come on baby. Take the dick!" he said slamming it in again this time managing to get most of his nine inches in. Tall at five eleven she was not exactly thick but it was obvious that if she wasn't a virgin that she hadn't had a lot of experience. Slamming it in further with each coldhearted thrust he could feel her getting wetter and wetter. She was meeting his thrusts now lifting her ass off the bed with each thrust.

"Damn you Anthony! Is that all you got? I said I want to feel you."

Anthony felt as though she was attacking his manhood now—telling him to bring it when he was tappin' that ass harder than he had ever had any woman. The sweat poured off of him and still she begged for more.

"Fuck me harder Anthony. Make this pussy purr. Make it remember you baby. Autograph it and make it yours baby. C'mon baby! Fuck my tight little pussy."

Anthony was groaning now.

"Is it good to you baby? You like this tight little pussy don't you?"

Anthony nodded.

"Tell me it's good baby."

"It's good Sammy."

"How good is it Anthony?"

"It's beautiful baby."

"Show me how beautiful it is baby. Take it out and taste it baby. Show me how much you appreciate it. Stop now and taste it. Make love to it baby. Make it good baby. Do it nice and slow. Make love to it baby. Make my pussy purrrrrr."

Pulling back on her elbows Samantha escaped Anthony's attempts to come. Then sitting up she grabbed him by the shoulders and forced him to his knees before grabbing his head and guiding it back to her throbbing pussy.

"Gently," she whispered.

Several hours later the two lay spent in each other's arms.

"I'd always envisioned this night," Samantha confessed but I must admit you far surpassed all expectations I had. You know it's funny but I half envisioned you as one of those half assed, stuffed shirt, Uncle Tom's when I first met you."

"And?"

"Well, I watched you and after a few weeks I noticed that you had a little swag with you. You know the kind the brothas have uptown."

"Is that right?"

"Don't you patronize me Anthony Pendleton. You have to admit that most of the brothas down on Wall Street are just unbleached White boys. Half of them act Whiter than their counterparts."

"I can't argue with you there but not being Black I guess you don't have or know the intricacies and dynamics of making it in a predominantly White subculture. What the brothers are doing is assimilating. Don't they have sociology at Wharton," he jabbed. Everyone knew that Samantha had attended the very prestigious Wharton School of Business and graduated at the top of her class but why she chose the lowly occupation of administrative assistant was beyond everyone's comprehension. Samantha playfully punched William in the side.

"Don't get smart Anthony."

Anthony laughed before continuing.

"Seriously though when the White man looks at a Black man in today's society he looks at him through jaded glasses. You know stereotypically. And if we don't take off the glasses then he's a criminal, a rapper, and basically a blight on society. So, in order for a brotha to halfway make it he has to assimilate or take on an alter ego to be accepted. Now a brotha that knows from early on—say high school—that this is where he wants to be and what he wants to do starts at an early age. He starts emulating those around him and often times loses himself sostrong is his need to make it and be accepted."

"Okay I get that. But how did you manage to remain loyal and true."

Anthony laughed.

"We all assimilate. We all play the role to some degree to make it. I was fortunate enough to have two parents that were activists in the movement and who would never let me forget my uniqueness, my Blackness. I guess that's what separates me from the rest. Well, that and the fact that my role models weren't Mitchell and Ness but some of the cool, intellectual brothers that I grew up with right here in the city."

"But why is it that you don't have to play that shufflin' Step and Fetch it role like them?"

"Can't rightly call it. Like you I graduated at the top of my class and as you know the only thing that's respected on the strip is money and being that I'm pretty proficient at turning a dime into fifteen cents they have to accept me for who I am. As long as I'm the goose laying the golden egg all is right with me. And then it becomes a thing of Mitchell and Ness assimilating or acquiescing to my demands."

"So,it would seem."

"What's that mean?"

"Well you and I and a lot of other people besides us recognize the fact that they should have made you a partner a long time ago."

"You sound like my wife now."

"Come on Ant. Your wife and I both say the same thing. And we both love you and wouldn't see any harm come to you. Then you know there must be some truth in it."

"I didn't say anything to the contrary. But she's putting the full court press on me around leaving Mitchell and Ness and opening up my own firm."

"Oh, Anthony. That's wonderful. When are you going to do it? You know that that's Mr. Mitchell's biggest fear. The word in the grapevine is that he's afraid that you're going to leave and take all of your clients with you. And you know if you were to do that that would be the end of Mitchell and Ness. I've always wondered why they just didn't bring you in as a partner and save themselves the trouble of losing you and possibly the firm."

"Must be the other class you missed at Wharton."

"What's that smart ass?"

"Racism 101. If Mitchell and Ness brought me in as a partner do you know how much flack they'd receive from the board members? And not just the board but from the other brokers who have been with the firm for years. There are brokers like Joe DiNardi and Mike Torelli who were with the firm when I was just a little tike in grade school. Not only would there be hell to pay from inside the firm but also up and Wall Street. Mitchell and Ness would be blamed for integrating the last bastion of White supremacy in an predominantly all-White institution."

"Okay, so then what you're telling me is that you have no choice but to open up your own firm."

"Is it just women or is it just the women I fall for?"

"And what's that supposed to mean?"

"I truly believe there's an emotional naiveté inherit in the genetic makeup of the x chromosome. There is a minor thing that both of you have failed to look at."

"And what's that professor?"

"That there is such a thing as a start up cost with any business. I don't care if you're selling lemonade."

"Okay and I'm missing your point as I'm sure Syl did. That wouldn't even be considered a factor being that your job is centered on making other people money. And if you're as proficient as you are at building other people's portfolios then it should be no problem accruing the monies needed for your own ventures."

"Well said Sammy and I by no means mean to appear to be facetious but if that's the case then under your guise there shouldn't be anything but wealthy stockbrokers on the floor."

"Come on Anthony. Don't patronize or play me for a fool I am quite aware that there are different echelons when it comes to brokers and although there are those that are not where you are for the normal little guy on the street fifty or sixty grand a year ain't nothing to shake a stick at. But we ain't talkin' about the average or below average brokers. We're talking about Anthony Pendleton, one of the hottest brokers on the strip and if you were to play your cards right and politic a little you should be able to come up with a mil five in no more than six months."

Anthony chuckled as Samantha wrapped the plush terry cloth robe around her.

"Damn, you came good. I have cum running all down my leg. I was kinda hopin' you had some left for a sort of nightcap but with the way this is running down my leg I'm not all that sure."

Anthony ignored her although he couldn't help but hear the steady beat of urine as it hit the water.

The two women closest to him both saw him as the inheritor of the firm, as the keeper of the flame and whereas Syl really didn't know Samantha was on the inside. A graduate of Wharton Samantha knew as much about trading as any of the brokers so if she told Ant that it was conceivable he was more inclined to agree because she handled his accounts and was familiar with the market.

"Can I ask you something Sammy?"

"Sure baby," Samantha said snuggling up into the crook of Anthony's armpit.

"Just a question that's been on the minds of most of the people at the firm including myself."

"And what's that?"

"Please tell me why someone who graduates from one of the top business schools in the country come to work at a firm as an administrative assistant which is no more than a glorified secretary?"

Samantha got up and made her way to the bar where she poured two glasses of wine. Handing one to Anthony she sat down on the bed Indian style and lit a cigarette before leaning over and kissing him long and hard. Sipping the wine slowly she stared at Anthony.

"When I first enKingd at Wharton I had all intentions of following my father's lead. He was an accountant and I was his precious little princess. Talk about a family man. My father had two possessions that he considered priceless. One was my mother and the other happened to be yours truly. He was a good provider and always appeared happy at least around me he did and he went to give me the best of everything. Anyway, he prodded me to go to Wharton and since my daddy wanted me to and I wanted daddy to be happy I applied and was accepted. I was young and didn't really know what I wanted to do so a career in business finance was as good as any other I guessed. I was just finishing my first semester as a senior when I got a call from my mother saying that my dad was seeing a therapist or shrink. I don't know but she said it was due to work related stress. I was only then that I found out how much my father hated his job. The only reason he stayed with it was for my mother and me but the whole time it was killing him and he never let on. A week later my mother called to inform me that my father had committed suicide."

"Oh no. Sammy I'm so sorry."

"Not half as sorry as I was. He left his little girl a note and the note read a little something like this. 'The quality of life can not me measured in dollars and cents. Find something that makes you happy and will afford you the same type of lifestyle that you are accustomed to. I love you more than life itself princess.' So, I took that as meaning that I should find something other than business and have shied away from it ever since."

"Okay you stop me if I'm crossing the line and getting too personal."

Samantha crushed the Marlboro out in the ashtray and stared at Anthony with those big blue-piercing eyes.

"Why stop now? I don't think you can get any more personal than having your face pressed into my pussy. And since we're on the subject when you finish with your questioning feel free to revisit my feel good. I haven't had it worked like that in God knows when and Lord knows it missed it."

"I may be able to do that."

"May? You will do that. You owe me that much Anthony."

"I owe you?" Anthony asked incredulously.

"Yes, you owe me for what I'm going to help you do."

"And what's that?"

"I'm going to invest in your future. That is I'm going to invest in your future and mine with a few stipulations."

Anthony smiled.

"And how do you know that's what I want to do?"

"Because I know my Anthony. And as much as you enjoy the security of Mitchell and Ness you need more. If it's one thing I've learned about you over the years Anthony is that complacency annoys you. You like movement. A mistake is not at all bad in your eyes. It's simply an opportunity, a chance taken that didn't necessarily meet with the desired results but that's okay as long as the effort was sincere and you availed yourself of the possibility. That's a trait you find with artists not financial analysts. But that's what separates the movers and shakers, the big boys, the all-stars from the rest of the pack."

"Is that right," Anthony said sarcastically.

"You know I'm right. You can patronize me all you want but you know what I'm saying is right on point. And you're not one of those that can just sit back and be complacent."

Putting his drink down he turned and stared into the blue eyes he now so detested for their piercing ability to see all that was inside his heart and soul.

"Perceptive is too kind a word. The words that come to mind right through here are hardly as flattering but it's been such an enjoyable evening I'm going to give you a pass."

Samantha laughed.

"Oh, I get it now. Big time stockbroker's wife is out of town and he's a little tired of the wife who's aging a little faster than even he expected. Now he's at a crossroads in his marriage and he's in a quandary especially when she's taking on the motherly role and wants to push him to realize his potential. So, he decides to relieve a little pressure and at the same time see if he's still got it by taking his fine ass little blonde secretary to one of the finest hotels in the city and bonin' the shit outta her letting her see how the other half lives at the same time. There's only one slight problem. Mr. Big Time has taken his little blonde secretary for granted as being just another dumb blonde and she's pushing him in the same way his wife is to realize his upside and now he's wondering if there's a conspiracy and truly wonders if there any peace," she laughed as she gulped down the rest of the rose and got up to refill both their glasses.

"I'm not even gonna dignify that by responding. I'm going to attribute those remarks to the alcohol. But I will respond to your previous remarks. You said you had a proposal."

"I do. I'll have it on your desk first thing in the morning. But enough talk. Come and make love to me my love."

Chapter 3

"Sylvia baby!? You look absolutely ravishing? What's it been about five years? Damn the years have been good to you," William remarked a smile pinned across his rounding, middle-aged face.

"Well, thank you love. Looks like marriage has agreed with you too. I never thought I'd see the day when William Stanton would be coordinated from head to toe."

William laughed.

"I see that tongue is still sharp as ever."

"I've mellowed a bit."

"I would like to believe that," he said ushering her to a table. "But even if you have you're still one hard nut to crack."

"I think you could have used a better choice of words to describe me."

"What can I say? I've known a few women in my day but not one that compares with you."

"I'm trying to make this a positive meeting of old friends," she smiled, "but you're certainly not making it easy."

"Easy has never been in your vocabulary baby. You don't do easy. You're high maintenance. Always have been. Always will be. But that's not to say that you don't push yourself as hard as you push the people you care about. But truth of the matter is you will succeed and the people around you are going to succeed or they'd better step the fuck off."

"Think you know me don't you?"

"I studied you more after our divorce than I did while I was in our marriage. Think that was part of the problem."

"You think?"

"Yeah, it was one of the things I had to work out. I honestly don't believe I've ever loved a woman as much as I loved you but maybe I was too young or insecure to realize it at the time."

"Having regrets?"

"Not really. I think it's a little late for that. But I do realize what you were trying to do for me and have tried to encompass most of your philosophy and I have to attribute a good deal of my success to that. That's why I send you a check on the regular. File it under a hard lesson learned but I prefer to call them consulting fees."

"Is that so. I thought it was 'cause I was a good fuck." Sylvia said smiling broadly now.

"That too but I'm dead serious. You're the best consultant I have without a shadow of a doubt."

"Well if that's the case then you should be all in for the proposition I'm about to put on the table."

And without further ado Sylvia laid out the proposal for the first predominately Black brokerage firm on Wall Street. William, ever attentive listened closely without interruption. When she was finished he sat back in his chair and reflected before summoning the elderly waitress and ordering another carafe of Zinfandel.

"I see you've thought it out pretty thoroughly and done your homework."

"Don't I always? Come on William. You know me. I always come correct. I wouldn't think of running this thing by the mayor and other especially if I didn't have the shit together. But this is no gamble by any stretch of the imagination. This is a sure thing just waiting to happen."

William chuckled.

"Same old Syl and listen, I believe in you Syl. I always have but let me play devils advocate for a minute. For half a mil I think I'm entitled to do that. Wouldn't you agree?"

"I gotcha. Fire away."

"How many Black brokerage houses are there?"

"Not many. To be honest outside of yours I don't really know of any. '

"That's because there are fewer than ten and do you know why that is."

"To be honest I can't say that I do."

"It's something I've given a considerable amount of thought to and without sounding to Cornel West like and to put it succinctly it's simply because this is a capitalistic society before it is a democracy or anything else. And what capitalism essentially is the fact that money controls everything and those with the capitol are White men and they will give up their very lives before they give up a dollar."

"That's understood William. I believe I was the one that helped bring that to your attention. But the fact remains that you are an example of someone that overcame the odds and made inroads into those all-White institutions and succeeded."

William laughed.

"Yeah, I guess you can say that but at what cost? I lost my wife, my boss and a little of my soul with that acquisition. And looking at you right now I know that all the money, prestige and power that I gained wasn't worth losing you."

"Do you mean that William?"

"With all my heart and soul. But anyway what you're attempting to undertake is a far cry from what I did so don't consider me the model."

"But sweetheart you are living proof that these things are conceivable."

"They are conceivable. But you have to look at things in the proper context. Don't mix apples and oranges.

Not only do you have to pick your battles you also have to pick your battlefields. Chill for a second and think back. Do you remember going to the Duke game when Shaq was still at LSU?"

Sylvia nodded yes to one of her fonder memories.

"Do you remember commenting about how the Duke fans were damn near on the court and how the only other Blacks you saw other than us was that lone cheerleader and the few Black players Duke had? You asked me how Shaq or any other player was supposed to thrive in a situation like that and before you got that sentence out Shaq was on the bench with three fouls. They weren't going to let Shaq, perhaps the most dominating center in the game of basketball, come into their house and make noise."

"And your point?"

"My point is that Shaq could have dominated on his home court but he wasn't going to go to Cameron Indoor Stadium and dominate anything. They weren't going to let him. Duke is the last bastion of so-called White supremacy in a Black dominated sport and the powers that be are going to keep it that way."

"So you're saying that the odds you had to overcome are obtainable but the one's Anthony has to overcome are not. Don't you think that's a little egotistical?"

William laughed.

"You always did have a way of twisting shit around. Don't take it personal." William said sipping the Zinfadel slowly. "All I'm saying is that the playing fields are different Syl. I'm here in what a lot of people call the New South. I started out in Atlanta. We play a large role in ever facet of life in Atl but New York is not Atlanta. Atlanta is small potatoes in comparison. We practically own Atlanta but as late as the '90's Blacks still didn't own real estate in Manhattan. That's not by accident Syl. And Wall Street is the financial capitol of the nation and the last outpost for White America. They're not letting Blacks in without a huge cost to whoever's trying to buck the odds. Can it be done? Hell yeah but you'd better be ready to pay the price is all I'm trying to say."

"Then you'll back us?"

"For a considerable piece of the pie,

he said. There was no smile on his face as he spoke.

"And what does that mean?"

"For ten per cent and a seat on the board."

"William?!?!"

"Listen Syl, I'm a businessman first and foremost and if and when you pull this coup off I want to be in on the ground floor."

"But William we're just getting started."

"One of the costs of getting started. Draw up a contract, making me a minority partner at ten per cent with an option to pick up another thirty to thirty five percent in the next ten years and a lifelong board member and I'll have my lawyers a detailed proposal and if all goes well and they like what they see and I agree that it's a good and profitable undertaking I'll have a check on the table by the following week give or take a day."

"Oh, come on William. At thirty five per cent and a seat on the board you'd have the board members eating out of your hand and be in a prime position to buy us out or simply stage a coup to take over. With your savvy and political connections you'd be able to sway the board and pull the rug out from under Anthony in a matter of months."

William chuckled.

"And you think I'd do that to you precious?"

"Think? I know you'd do it. What is it you used to say? Money over bitches."

William laughed aloud.

"That was a long time ago Syl."

"That was a long time ago. The terminology may have changed but the fact remains the same. Now you just say it's business. Nothing personal. Different words. Same results."

"Is that right?"

"You've always been shrewd William but please—this is for me—a sort of favor baby. We're a mom and pop organization just trying to get started, trying to get our feet wet and we can't afford an internal coup or even have to worry about internal strife when we have to worry about all the big guns aiming our way and trying to destroy us. What we need starting off is a unified and cohesive front. No internal threats. Anthony's no politician. I'm hoping he grows into the role but at present he's not equipped for you and your cunning.

"Sweetheart, believe me I'm not close to being the threat that Anthony is about to encounter when word gets out that an African American has plans on invading their last stronghold of White America."

"So, what you're telling me is that you wouldn't pull the rug from under us once we get it up and running."

"Have I ever done anything to hurt you sweetheart?"

"You married Melinda."

William ignored the comment.

"So what is it exactly that you want from me Syl?"

"What I want is for you to invest in us and lend us your firm's name and support for credibility. I'd also like for you to act as a sort of part time consultant on a per diem basis to guide Anthony through the rough waters."

"Not to be pessimistic but that's going to be a full time gig. Forget about the per diem basis."

"And for my time and trouble?"

"Let's go with the ten per cent cut and dry as a favor to me. If all goes well and by my estimations that should result into three quarters of a mil to a mil in about five years."

"Sounds good but you haven't mentioned what kind of investment in dollars you're looking for. I'm sure that was just an oversight on your part but it does have some bearing on my agreeing to your terms or not."

"Oh, I'm sorry William thought I had."

Sylvia then drew a piece of paper and a pen from her purse and scribbled quickly before sliding it across the table to William. William amused by Sylvia's actions smiled briefly before opening the paper.

"Have you lost your damn mind? Even if I were to consent I could never get those kind of numbers past the board of directors. A million five is a major investment even if it were an established firm but an investment like that in an unproven commodity is if nothing else risky and people in my business take very few risks. And most of my board being White are still having a hard time dealing with me CEO so you can imagine what kind of reception I'd get if I were to put forth a proposal for a million five to start an African American brokerage firm on Wall Street."

"But if you truly believe in us William you know you can veto their say with or without the boards approval."

"You're right but it's not something I'd be apt to do. Many of our clients look at the board as a reason to invest in us and to usurp their authority would be tantamount to treason—almost like you're nothing more than a face and reputation and since I can't go where you can as a Black or have the political clout and connections I'm simply using you to do my bidding for me."

"Well that's the truth isn't it?"

"To a degree it is but it's much more than that. Last May for instance when we considered the takeover of Jacob and Miller the board was split right down the middle. I listened to both sides and they were both adamant concerning the pros and cons of the takeover. I was the deciding vote and I decided against it because there were too many things that just weren't right with the deal. I had too many unanswered questions. And when you are not absolutely sure it's best to play it safe. I'm sure you've since read about them going bankrupt and O'Bama having to bail them out."

"I have."

"And they were a proven commodity. They were founded in the late eighteen hundreds and were thriving during the late twenties and early thirties went the rest of the country was going up during the Great Depression. But anyway that's what the board went through with a proven institution. What the hell do you think there reaction would be when I mention a lone broker is trying to open his own firm? And granted they know of Anthony's proficiency on Wall Street. But no Syl, I can tell you right now that shit for that type of money ain't gonna fly."

"Not even with the backing of Mutual of Life and the mayor lending their support."

"That may be fine in our community if you're looking for financial support but not in the financial community I represent. You'd need people like Bill Gates or someone like Romney—businessmen who are tried and true to invest to lend some credibility."

"Then can you see fit to come out of your own pocket to invest in us William?"

William chuckled.

"I have a board of directors of one and she's every bit as tough as those I work for but it's still going to cost you."

"Ain't nothin' free. Didn't expect it to be. But I offered you a ten percent share in the company holdings. What more can I offer you?"

"William smiled again.

"I can think of a few things," he said glaring at her cleavage. "Let me see just how much this means to you and I can better judge how much of a risk I'm taking."

"Name it William."

"Meet me at the Hilton Hotel in Charlotte at nine sharp. You get the room and in the meantime I'll fax your proposal to my layer and have him take a quick look. And while he's looking it over I'll run it by Melinda and see what she says. I'll let you know the verdict when I see you."

And with that William stood up before bending over and kissing Syl on the cheek and turning and leaving the now empty restaurant.

On the drive to Charlotte Syl had plenty of time to think and reflect. She thought about her marriage and her drugging and sexual tryst with Mayor Booker while he was unconscious. And now here she was about to sell her soul to the devil again. She knew William well enough to know that his propositions somehow always involved sex. Even when they'd been married and played Scrabble he'd bet and when she lost which she inevitably did he would always require sex as payment. At first she hated losing with her overly competitive nature but after he'd administered the good good she in time would inevitably lose on purpose though she would never let him know that was the case. To her it was a win win situation even when she lost. But that was then. Now she wondered how far she'd come when a few hundred thousand would cause her tolie down with a man to help better her situation. She could remember better days. The days when men would offer her and try to buy her just to make themselves a fixture in her life but now she was the aggressive one and what was even worse was the fact that she did it with the hopes of enriching her husband's fortune. But then there was nothing wrong with that. After all, there was no one who'd ever loved her more. So, and how others perceived her didn't matter as long as Anthony was happy and reached his aspirations.

Recalling briefly she remembered as a bit of a freak when it came to the bedroom and wondered just what he had in mind tonight but for a million five she could easily heal from whatever he put her through. Besides it was only a night and all he probably wanted to do was reminisce of days gone by.

Chapter 4

Samantha rose from the bed after what seemed like forever stood up. Every inch of her hurt and yet she smiled as she made her way to the bathroom. The urine stung her torn pussy and she smiled. She'd finally had the opportunity to sleep with the man she'd man she fantasized about for the last five and a half years and despite being sore and hurt she had no regrets. She'd put in for a half a day today with just this in mind and after fixing a hotel pot of coffee she went back to bed and lit a cigarette. Inhaling deeply she felt her chest rise and fall with each breath. Even her chest hurt as she stared at the ceiling grinning.

'Brotha can really lay it down', Samantha said as she reminisced recalling each moment from the past night. 'Wonder how he'll react today when he sees me? I wonder what kind of impression I left with him if any. I wonder if he'll play me off like last night never happened or if he'll embrace me in some sort of way to let me know he appreciated me. He may look at me in another light now. Then again he could look at last night like just another carefree one night stand.' Samantha' attitude suddenly changed and she wondered how she should proceed. She had always given him a hundred and ten percent of her at work. And last night she'd given him her the rest of him. She could remember her dear father, God rest his soul, remarking to her one day that if she gave expecting something in return she hadn't really given anything at all. It was with that thought that she put the night in perspective and began to prepare for the day ahead. The first thing on the agenda was to draw up a contract that she thought both fitting and fair to both and with nothing so much as a reference to last night. Strictly business it could only reflect her business interest. And after five years of coordinating and compiling Anthony Pendleton's client's portfolios she was quite aware of his financial prowess. And in her meager meanderings with the other secretaries she was quite aware of the talk around Mitchell and Ness. She made it a point to always stay in earshot and after awhile became close friends with Mr. Mitchell's wife who also doubled as his administrative assistant and right hand man when Mr. Ness' health failed. It was from Anne that she really learned how valuable and indispensable Anthony was to the firm. Samantha remembered it like it was yesterday. After an extended lunch which started with a Apple martinis sandwiched by a brief shopping spree to Neiman

Marcus and Sak's they'd returned to Commuter's Café and sipped more Apple martini's into late in the afternoon. When it was all over she learned that Anthony Pendleton had grossed over sixty million in his then seven years with the firm. 'A valuable asset,' Anne had commented. 'It was such a shame he was a Negro. Oh, the places he could have gone if he'd just been born White. Still, he is one handsome boy colored boy. I've never had a colored boy. Have you?' Samantha appalled at the woman's remarks shook her head no but the woman's words haunted her until this day as she recounted Mrs. Mitchell's words. 'A White man would have left Mitchell and Ness a long time ago, maybe even started his own house but where can that poor boy go. There are no Black brokerage houses. And even if there were I don't think he would go. That's one I give colored folks credit for. When you find a good one they're the most loyal folks you can find. In Anthony's case he realizes that there aren't a lot of his color down on Wall Street and he realizes that Mr. Ness gave him the opportunity of a lifetime and that's why he's so thankful for the opportunity. He realizes that he's one of only a handful of Negroes that earns a six figure salary and he's grateful. Most of his kind are out there robbing and stealing just trying to put food on the table and he knows it. And that's why he doesn't say a peep. It's because he understands what a privileged place my husband has put him in.'

Samantha never uttered a word. She was tempted to tell Anthony but was unsure of s response and she'd hate to have to train a new boss. Besides they worked so well together she felt no need to disrupt perfection. And he was so lenient and laid back, never finding the need to micro manage but giving her space and constantly complimenting her on her efficiency that she for fear of getting someone else not nearly so compatible made the decision not to repeat Anne

Mitchell's bigoted words. That very same night she called her mother and was surprised to hear her mother wax so poetically on the subject.

"Sammy as long as there is a world we will have all types of people and in those different types of people there will always be a segment that is ignorant, less informed and enlightened. It is our job to enlighten and inform when and where we can and to ignore those that seek to remain stagnant and steadfast in their ignorance. This woman sounds like one of the people that should simply be ignored. It's a shame that a woman of this magnitude cannot and is not in a better place because with all of her money and power she could certainly be an effective agent for change."

She'd hung up the phone feeling somewhat better and was convinced at that point of two things. One was that she would do everything in her willpower to aid Anthony Pendleton shine and overcome the odds that were inherent in his being denied his just due because of his skin color. The other thing she was convinced of was that she was in love with Anthony Pendleton. And from that day forth she was the crutch he needed to cross the wide barrier of racism that denied him a promotion and partnership in Mitchell and Ness.

Two hours later, Samantha glanced at her phone. It was ten after ten and she had already completed her contract and faxed it to her mother who had a law degree but had failed to take the bar when she became pregnant with Samantha. Showering quickly Samantha's ravaged body still ached. She'd planned on taking a long hot bath but the time had once again eluded her. By the time she arrived at work it would be close to twelve. She'd always prided herself on being punctual and today would be no different. After last night she wanted to appear even more businesslike than usual. Samantha donned her black double-breasted suit with black Manolo Blahniks to boot. The looks she garnered on her way to the subway only established her attempts at being sensual yet elegant. A half an hour later Samantha reached the office and was surprised to find herself a tad bit nervous. She had to begrudgingly admit that she hadn't felt this way since her initial interview some five years earlier. Damn! She had been in control dictating the evening and she had commanded his discipline and obedience so there was no reason for her to feel this way. Sure, she had given herself to a married man being fully aware of the implications and consequences of her actions so why was she worried. Getting off the elevators at the twenty-first floor she suddenly felt her stomach contract as she headed down the long hallway to her office. Two rather distinguished Black gentlemen sat in the outer office. Putting her pocketbook in the bottom desk drawer she spoke.

"Gentleman. Is someone taking care of you?"

"We just arrived but no no one's taking care of us," the forty-ish gentleman with the nattily attired suit and trench coat replied.

"And you're here to see Mr. Pendleton?"

"Yes, just let him know that two of his old college buddies dropped by to see him."

"Will do. Just give me a second," Samantha took a deep breath and could feel the men's eyes on her as she went and knocked on Anthon's door.

"Who?"

"Samantha."

"Come in."

Samantha walked in closing the door behind her.

"Ooooh Sammy! Goodness lady! You look even better than you did last night and I swear I didn't believe that was possible. " he said moving past her and leaning against the door to prevent any unwanted visitors. With his back against the door he grabbed her wrists and pulled her towards him.

"When I left you this morning and got to the office I asked myself how'd I react when you came in? I promised myself that I'd be professional and keep up a respectable demeanor for the sake of protocol but now that I see you all that is history."

Anthony's words eased Samantha's worst fear and for the first time since she'd left the hotel she was at ease.

"I feel the same way but let's keep it professional while we're here Anthony. Besides we have too much on the agenda today. Let's focus on the task at hand."

"You're right," he said kissing her gently as she pushed him away.

"You have two guests waiting to see you in the reception area. They claim to be old college buddies."

"Oh, those would be might frat brothers D'Andre and MJ. Would you send them in?"

"And I'm putting my offer we talked about last night on your desk for you to look over when you get a chance."

"I'll do that the first chance I get and let you know just as soon as I do. Please send them in. Oh, and by the way could you please check and see if I have any other appointments this afternoon? If there's nothing imperative I want to be out of here by four. I have some personal things I need to take care of."

"Gotcha. I'll do what I can to push everything back 'til tomorrow," she said exiting the office.

"Mr. Pendleton will see you now," Samantha said to the two gentlemen who rose and entered through the still open door.

"What's good Blackman?" MJ said embracing Anthony as if he were a long lost brother returning from the war.

"My God it's good seeing you two. Been down here in this desert so long I forgot what it is to be around the brothers."

"Fuck the brothers when you got somethin' that fine waitin' on you hand and foot all day every day," Malik Jamal commented.

"Thought you were Muslim?" Anthony remarked. "Ain't that blue-eyed devil the reason we in the situation we in today."

"You right. You right. I'm Muslim from the top of my head right on down to my waist. Past that I'm Christian willing to forgive and forget all," he laughed. "Shit for something as fine as that I'd forget religion altogether."

"You know every Blak man's dream is a White woman," D'Andre laughed. "She don't have to be fine or nothin'. Long as she's White."

"And you got both fine and White. Shit, no disrespect but I know Syl's ass is on the auction block."

"You're stupid," Anthony laughed, "You ain't changed a bit since college."

"You know people don't change. They just get older. I've been trying to convert D'Andre since he was a freshman in college but he still love bacon and White women.   You know I joke but he's serious into that. Always has been. Thought his eyes was gonna fall out when he saw Sammy."

"Ah, nigga you was lookin' too."

"Couldn't help it. Allah gave me sight to view the beauty he created and I'm damn well gonna take it all in. And Lord knows there ain't much more beautiful than that fine specimen of a woman you call your secretary. That's all I know."

"You right about that my brotha. But tell me honestly Ant. Is you hittin' that or not."

"You fools are still crazy after all these years," Anthony laughed.

"But is you hittin' it?"

"Lord no. I've been happily married for going on eleven years now and there ain't no need for me to get married if I wanted to hit everything with a fat ass and a pretty face."

"You right. You right and Syl is fine. Well, she was fine the last time I saw her but that was at your wedding ten years ago and she had crows feet then. The way I figure it she must be completely gray and wrinkled by now. No disrespect Ant and you know you my boy but I never did understand why you married that old bat anyway. She looked like she was on the cusp of AARP when ya married her," All three laughed as Ant pulled out a bottle of Henny and three glasses and poured each of them a healthy double.

"Nah! None for me," Malik said waving Ant off.

"Ah, nigga stop frontin'," Malik said. "Ya love bacon and White women what's a lil Henny gonna do. Have a drink with yo' brothas. I'm tellin' ya Ant, half the time I don't recognize this brotha he got a house over in Jersey and every time I see him he try to get new on me."

"Is that right," Ant said smiling and sipping the Henny.

"Ain't nothin' wrong with D ceptin' he henpecked."

"How's Charisse doing anyway," Anthony asked.

"She's good. Couldn't be better. You know she's expecting again."

"She's always expecting. Every time you look up she's expecting. I don't see how the nigga has time to make babies 'cause she works him like a dog. When he comes home she slobs on his knob spreads them little fat legs til she's pregnant and then sends him out to make some more money while she makes more kids. Nigga in so deep and so blind that he don't know whether he's comin' or going. Let me tell you how fucked up he is Ant. We went out to lunch over at this place in the Ironbound section of Newark or was it East Orange? I can't rightly recall but in any case. I ordered two juicy porterhouse steaks for us and he damn near came on hisself talkin' bout he ain't never tasted nothin' so good in all his life so I wait a couple of days and call him and tell him to meet me there and he tells me he can't go. Now we ate there on Monday and on Wednesday when I call him back the niggas a vegan. I'm tellin' ya Ant this nigga done changed. Charisse done not only pussy whipped the brother she done brainwashed his ass too."

Anthony sat there with tears running down his face while D'Andre tired of defending himself simply said 'fuck you'.

A knock on the office door subdued the laughter.

"Don't stop on my account," Samantha said cordially as she stuck her in the door.

"I would stop the world on your account sweetheart," Malik countered.

Samantha smiled but did not bother to respond. It was quickly apparent that she was used to this.

"Yes Sammy?"

"Just wanted you to know that I cleared your schedule for this afternoon. Pushed everything back to tomorrow and next Monday. The afternoon is yours."

"Thanks Samantha."

"Not a problem," she replied before closing the door and returning to her desk.

"On the real, what's Syl think of her?"

"You know come to think of it she's never even mentioned her."

"All jokes aside, Syl's a tough woman. If she doesn't consider Samantha a threat she is one tough sista, secure in herself. I know a lot of sistas would have made you get rid of her just on gp."

"You ain't lying about that," D'Andre agreed. "Charisse would have said she's gotta go."

"Hell, the way Charisse looks Scooby Doo is a threat," Malik replied. No maliciousness intended the two had been going at it since high school and being that it was all in good natured kidding and the two were as close as blood brothers it had become accepted.

"C'mon let's get out of here," Anthony said filling both their glasses and his own before downing it and grabbing his overcoat. The two gentleman followed his lead grabbing their coats, draining their glasses and following him out of the office.

"Hold the fort down Sammy. I'll be back in a couple of hours to talk to you about your proposal. If you get tired of waiting go ahead home but I shouldn't be any later than three thirty, four at the latest."

"Nice meeting you both."

"Same here," both men said in unison before exiting the plush offices of Mitchell and Ness.

"So, what's with all the urgency?"

"Just wanna let my brothas get in on the ground floor of something good. Gonna give you a chance to make some real money," Anthony said.

"I'm listening," D'Andre said as he hailed a cab.

"C'mon let's head uptown to Sylvia's. I feel like some fried chicken."

"Nah, I can't do it. I have to read this proposal Samantha gave me to read before she goes home or she'll have my head."

"You sure ain't nothin' goin' on there?" Malik asked. "You one of the few brothas I ain't never worried about crossing the line but in her case I couldn't fault you if you did."

"No really, seriously, on the real, ain't nothin' happenin'," Anthony replied more or less pleading his case. He hadn't seen Malik or D in close to a year and it was important that they keep their view of him as it had always been and especially now when he needed them both to make a sizeable contribution into a venture he was not all that sure of himself. It was more important now than it had ever been in the fifteen or so years that he knew them that they see him as a pillar of decency, a cornerstone of what they believed the new Blackman to be and he didn't want to do anything to dispel their belief in him.

"As long as she's blonde haired and blue eyed all she can ever be is my secretary," he said nonchalantly. "Let's shoot over to Juniors. I can go for a chicken salad sandwich and a piece of their cheesecake." He hoped this would change the conversation and both men realizing they were hungry, agreed. Once in Juniors Anthony laid out his plan for his boys who both agreed to support him. Malik agreed that it was important for Blacks to finally get a foothold in every facet of American society and the financial aspect was as important as any avenue yet to be obtained. He went on to expound on how it was in direct correlation with the nation of Islam's need for the Black man to obtain the means to be self-sufficient to the point where D'Andre said if he didn't shut up with all his Black nationalism bullshit he was gonna shove the damn Reuben down his throat. Malik who now owned a chain of thirty-two coin operated Laundromats and car washes in the Tri-State area saw no problem with a meager sum of a hundred and fifty thousand at ten percent interest over the course of a year. D'Andre, a regional manager for Chase Manhattan committed to a similar sum but had to check with Charisse before he could make a decision. And despite Malik's teasing all present knew that whatever D'Andre decided Charisse would agree to. The two wrote checks right then and there and with them firmly in his grasp Anthony parted ways promising to meet them in a week to keep them abreast of his progress.

Following lunch Anthony headed back to the office. It was three fifteen. He'd told Samantha he'd be back by three-thirty and was cutting it close. Hoping she'd still be there he hailed a cab and read what he could of her proposal on the ride back.

By this time and after ten years of broken dreams fostered by false promises made by the firm that claimed they loved and appreciated his value to him he had to admit that Samantha wrote extremely well but he was also cautious. Syl was constantly reinforcing the fact that a little fear was a good thing. Calling him gullible and naive never sat well with him since he'd always considered himself streetwise but this was a new playing field and one that he knew little about and the possibility that she could be right bothered him even more. He'd done his best to hone his senses since then and felt he'd sharpened his Spidey senses where he could recognize the wool being pulled over his eyes or anything remotely resembling a con or a sham. Now here he was reading the proposal Sammy had drawn up it was hard to imagine her coming up with so an astute and detailed proposal in the short time she had since they'd parted earlier this morning. Either she was a genius well versed in the law—for there were little or no loopholes or she'd been prompted by someone in authority to make this maneuver. Whatever it was something just didn't sit well with him and before he proceeded further he'd have to have a sit-down, a face to face with her and make sense of the whole thing.

Arriving back at his office he was surprised to find Samantha still hard at work filing some clients paperwork and answering the phones. One thing was for sure, the girl was hardly lazy and he only wished he could infuse her work ethic into some of the teens he knew. There was no doubt she'd go far but it certainly wouldn't be at his expense.

"Sammy if you have a minute can I please see you in my office."

"On my way Mr. Pendleton."

"Have a seat."

It was as if the previous night had not existed at all for either of them. Now it was business as usual. And whereas they were usually on the same page something was different now and Samantha quickly sensed something had gone awry.

"What's wrong?" she said trying to appear cool and calm despite Anthony's noticeable change in attitude.

"Well, first of all I did get a chance to look over your proposal and I must say that you write extremely well. I hadn't realized just how well."

"Most law students do."

"My bad Sammy. I thought you told me you told me you were an accounting major."

"I did Anthony. I double majored. My other was law. But why all the questions. You make me feel like I'm being interrogated—like I'm under investigation for something I've done. Talk to me. I'm lost."

Anthony managed a smile.

"I'm sorry Samantha. It's just that I'm under a lot of stress right through here. Syl's putting a lot of pressure on me right through here about starting my own firm. I think she's even more anxious and disturbed about me being looked over here than I am and has given me an ultimatum. It's basically man up and start your own firm or step off. And then she leaves. I don't know if she misses the headlines, or she doesn't have enough money or she just wants to see me prosper and grow. I honestly don't know. So, I start feeling a little paranoid about the whole situation and decide to get away and just try to relax a little. Which leads me to last night.

For more than five years I watch my bright, young, vivacious secretary prance around in front of me while

I try my damndest to keep it as professional as possible. My back against the wall I decide to take some time and do me and so I proposition my secretary and my feelings are pretty much on point and mutual when she decides to join me. And to be perfectly frank she made me think about my marriage and even contemplate ending it. But then I start to confide in her as I always have. Only this time it's on a personal instead of a business level and she tells me that she' been thinking the same thing that my wife has been thinking. I have to wonder if it's a conspiracy. And then after making good love my pretty, young secretary comes at me with a verbal proposal. So, I tell her to put it in writing just to see if it's just a whim—you know—just trash talk in passing. And the net morning she has a five-page proposal sitting on my desk that is as detailed and clean as new falling snow. It's just all a little hard to perceive so I felt the need to address it in person and get the skinny on the whole situation."

Samantha was grinning from ear-to-ear.

"So you did think it was good Ant?"

"Awfully hard to believe you composed that this morning after I left you."

"Who said anything about composing anything this morning? You know what they say about assuming. Truth of the matter is that I am perceptive. And some time ago I watched you and your growth rate with Mitchell and Ness and became cognizant of your sales in relation to the other brokers. I kept my ear to the ground and learned a lot about the firm and you and the firm in relation to you. Then one day—and I swore I'd never tell you this—I went shopping and to lunch with Mrs. Mitchell. That day I was introduced to racism in corporate America. For two hours and too many drinks Mrs. Mitchell talked about you and your value to Mitchell and Ness. She also mentioned what a shame it was that you were Black and would never be able to climb the corporate latter and receive your just due because you were Black."

"She said that?"

"In so many words. I'm being somewhat more gracious than she was however."

"Wow," was all Anthony could muster.

"In any case, I was so utterly devastated that she who I really happened to like up until that day could be so ugly and mean in her hatred. So, I went home and thought about it and when it got too much for me to fathom I called my mother who gave me her version of the serenity prayer. But more importantly she told me not to mention the conversation and to come up with a plan that would aid you in your endeavors."

"And what did you come up with?"

"Well, in all actuality I didn't come up with anything as you can see. I tried to remain low key, which I guess you gathered last night is not my forte. But I was content to watch, listen, and learn and I heeded my daddy's words."

"And they are..."

"Both my parents started out as teachers. And my father's favorite two sayings were 'all things in time' which referred to biding your time and the other was to wait for an optimum teaching moment. That is you can have the knowledge to teach but are your students receptive; do they want to be taught because you feel the need to teach and are they listening when you do decide to teach? I had to bide my time with you and wait for the optimum teaching time to speak. I knew it would only be some time when you would recognize that Mitchell and Ness didn't have your best interest at heart and I knew—no disrespect intended—that with the diva you were married to you wouldn't have the funds to get started so I kept daddy's trust fund for me at bay 'til either you gave me a tip worth investing in or you saw fit to invest in yourself. So, as you can see Mr. Pendleton this wasn't something I drew up because the loving was all that—and it was—or because of some little conspiracy. It was just having the foresight to see what inevitably would transpire. Can't say they were for purely out of philanthropic purposes either. If I said that I'd be lying. I was looking for a career opportunity as well. In the five years I've worked for you I've been studying and following right along with each and every account and think I've become pretty proficient at being able to manage accounts and clients. And now that I've put some of daddy's ghosts to bed I think I'm ready to embark on what I initially set out to do."

"I see," was all Anthony could say mildly surprised at the sincerity of Sammy's words.

"Not only did I put together a contract proposal that will jumpstart my career but I've also coordinated a business plan and mission statement which will help your business get up and running with little or no flaws."

Anthony Pendleton couldn't help but smile. This little girl with the enormous I.Q. had not only studied him but had come up with a preemptive strike before he had even thought about making a fight of it and he could hear his father's words as plain as day. 'Whites and women have one thing in common and it will serve to keep them both on top of the world for a while to come. And do you know what that is son?' Anthony would always shake his head no. 'Well I'll tell you what it is they have in common and what that is that will always keep us in second place trying to play catch up. Both of them know how to plan. And once they have a plan they act on it. They are proactive. We as men and I mean Black men wait til an injustice is undone, then waste time grappling with the unjustice and then after wrestling with it for far too long, decide to react to it. We've already lost the race by this point. We're reactive when we should be proactive. Anthony sat back at his desk and looked at Samantha. She'd watched the events unfold and planned a course of action while he who was on the hot spot had failed to pick up the baton even after it had been shoved into his hand.

"So, I was right. This proposal wasn't written this morning."

"I'm good Anthony but I'm not that good. Although I did send it to mommy to look over for any errors, mistakes or oversights on my part."

"And?"

"Haven't heard from her. Mommy's a busy lady with a life of her own. She wanted to be a lawyer so badly but was never ever able to take the bar when she got pregnant with me but she's the best lawyer I know without a practice."

"Tell me something seriously though Sammy. How long have you been sitting on this proposal?"

"I don't know," she said crossing her long legs revealing her rich, deep olive skin and her heavy almost Negroid thighs. Skinny could hardly describe the more than ample woman but there was no fat to be found on her more than well-endowed figure. Anthony sighed as she crossed her leg and thought of how she'd ridden him taking all that he had to give and how he would love to repeat the performance. Gathering himself he returned his gaze to her eyes but the pools of blue served him no better and unable to stay focused he proceeded to fill a pitcher with ice water.

"Come to think of it. I saw the handwriting on the wall that day I went to lunch with Mrs. Mitchell and started working a day or two later."

"And this is the result?"

"It is."

"And so what you're looking at is a sizeable loan with ten per cent interest accrued annually and an administrative assistants position similar to what you have here at close to twice your current pay with the guarantee that you will be promoted to an entry level broker and will be promoted at three month intervals based on merit until you reach the status of senior broker at which time you will be brought in front of the board and considered for a minority holding and possible partnership."

Anthony couldn't help but look up at Samantha from time-to-time. He'd read many a contract in his day but hadn't come across one with quite as many incentives and perks as hers had and was somewhat pleased.

"It's a little self-serving. Reminds me of a professional athletes contract with all the incentives," Anthony laughed.

"You're right it does but let me ask you this. Who prospers if Kobe Bryant or Kevin Garnett have break out seasons? Who really profits if Anthony Pendleton surpasses all his yearly goals and has a breakout season?"

"Mitchell and Ness."

"My point exactly. And who will be the real winner if Samantha King reaches all of her lofty ass goals. Well, no other than Pendleton and associates."

"I guess the only other thing that appears to be a little concerning is your investing though sizeable wants an inordinate return."

"Oh, come on Anthony ten percent of a company that hasn't gotten off the ground. A two hundred thousand dollar investment on a dream deferred for five years for lack of confidence that you can get it to fly and you want to complain about the ten per cent I think should be rightfully mine for investing in something you yourself don't have confidence in. Oh please. Get a grip Anthony. You know me and you damn sure know my capabilities so stop frontin'. Sign the damn and give it to me so we can get the damn thing rollin' and stop bullshittin'. You know it's precise and thorough just like the rest of me. Now sign it so I can get out of here."

Anthony smiled knowing that she was correct in her assessment but he was surprised with the tone she addressed him in.

"What's your rush?"

"It's been a long day and I have a date," Samantha replied matter-of-factly.

The look of dejection hung heavily on Anthony's face.

"Oh, stop looking so glum. I'm meeting mommy. Among other things she's a notary republic."

"And I'll meet you at the hotel around eight?"

"I would love to say yes but only if you change hotels."

"Change hotels? Why Sammy?" Anthony was confused. How could a woman from any ilk say no to the Ritz Carlton?

"Because you're trying to open a business and you're going to need all the money you can lay your hands on. Besides we're simple folk. I'm from Newark and you're from uptown. We don't need to try and impress one or another. I'm here for your company Ant. And it's only because I like you. Not the drapes in the hotel room."

"That's why I'm so crazy about you," Ant said squeezing her tightly despite her objections.

Later, that evening as Anthony drove over to Jersey his thoughts went back to Samantha.

She was beautiful but not in the Cosmopolitan magazine way. She was closer to a taller version of Marilyn Monroe, thick in all the right places and buxom to boot. Her ass full and round made Ant grinned just thinking about it and in the five years they'd been co-workers she had always been cordial, friendly and straightforward. She oozed both sensuality and sexuality and turned both many a client and coworkers head. But she had ignored them all staying true to herself and he in carrying out her daily functions. Whatever life she had outside of Mitchell and ness remained an enigma as she never spoke of home or her time off . That's the way it had been since her arrival and not even Syl could comment on the young woman's attitude and work ethic. That was up until yesterday when she'd agreed to meet him at the Ritz Carlton for a couple of drinks after another long hard tiring day. He'd found out more last night than he'd come to find out in the last five years and found himself enamored by her quiet frankness, her subdued intelligence and humility and during the course of the day found himself unconsciously comparing her to Syl.

He wondered if he were being too harsh on Syl. After all, she'd been his wife for close to a dozen years. He wondered if he'd married too soon and if he'd subconsciously been looking for a mother figure as the whispers emerged following their wedding. Perhaps his father's words were more apropos when he suggested that familiarity breed's contempt. Or perhaps he was simply a victim of success and much as he hated it falling prey to the rather common stereotype that suggested that suggested that soon as a brotha made it he was off in search of a White woman. Sure Syl had her flaws but then who didn't. At times she was aggressive and obnoxious and she was starting to age but then who wasn't. That was just an inevitable part of this thing called life and he'd only be fooling himself if he thought he could upgrade to a newer, younger model. In reality Syl had everything that a man could wish for. She was bright, articulate, with a body to die for and she knew how to use it and make him scream for mercy on command but there was something there and in twelve years he had never been able to quite put his finger on it but on several occasions she'd get up in the wee hours and walked around in an unconscious state and provide some bizarre scenarios. Most of the time she wouldn't remember a thing. She referred to them as night terrors and said they were common among children but at thirty-nine Anthony sensed something deeper, more troubling. But aside from a few quirks and being overindulgent, spoiled, and a nag at times she was everything a man could ask for. And yet now, for some reason she just wasn't enough. He found himself wanting and needing more if only for a change of place. Being with her he found himself growing complacent and the fear that he was losing some of his drive and spontaneity bothered him tremendously.

Mulling over the idea of monogamy he found more and more that with all of Syl's attributes he longed for his freedom. He was becoming more and more frustrated with the idea of checking in and being cognizant of everything he did and having someone tell him where he could go and what he could do when he did go. He hated when she told him that he couldn't drink and how to dress and just being—well—just being Syl. It would probably have been easier if he hadn't started seeing Samantha until he'd separated from Syl. But with the guilt came doubt. Was he separating because of Samantha? Or was it because he was truly tired of Syl and the idea of marriage? Among all the other things he had to deal with he didn't need any more problems but with the recurring thought of his marriage he knew something had to give soon. He was caught between two worlds, a world that despite her efforts had become mundane and common and another which held all the frivolity, freedom and spontaneity of life that could cause a man to sell his very soul to the devil. Sure Syl had been his loyal and caring wife for the past twelve years but as B. B. King had so promptly and adequately put it 'The Thrill Was Gone'. And yes in all his truthfulness she had been more than an adequate wife but at this moment in his life adequate somehow just wasn't good enough and since she had always been true to him he knew he owed it to her to be truthful and honest about his feelings now or lack thereof. Yes, he'd fought his feelings for far too long, long before Sam had entered the picture and in fact she had only been the icing on the cake. But now it was time to purge himself and in his honesty he would not only relieve himself of this weight but would be freeing her of trying to please a man that could not be pleased despite her constant and continuous efforts. The tears Kingd down Anthony's cheeks as he drove slowly down the West Side highway aimlessly rehearsing his lines. Not one to procrastinate he knew it best to tell Syl tonight before she go wind of his affair with Sam and before she put her and soul into investing in a man that could not reciprocate. And then out of weakness or second thoughts he made his way to the Holland Tunnel with tear stained eyes found his way to Sammy's. If anyone could offer him solace and a fitting way out it would be her. Wiping the tears from his eyes he tried to put on air of good cheer and rang her doorbell. The young woman who knew Anthony as well as anyone could see be beneath the thin disguise and immediately grabbed and pulled him to her bosom

"Anthony baby. What's wrong," she cried out in disbelief. In all the time she'd known him she'd never seen him so distraught and it was all a little disquieting to her. Still, whatever it was that was bothering him she was sure she could fix it and in a sense it gave her some pleasure knowing that he'd come to her first and foremost in his time of need.

"I just can't do it anymore Sammy. I just can't," he repeated, the tears once again flowing freely.

"Baby, you've got to talk to me. I'ma need you to be straight up and tell me what the hell is going on. I can't do anything for you if you don't talk to me. I'm gonna need you to be straight up with me. I'm not just anybody. If I were you wouldn't have come here but the only way we can get to the root of what's bothering you is by you laying it out on the line and then once you do that we can put our heads together and work out a solution."

"What's to work out? I'm just tired. What's there to work out? Don't you just ever just get tired? I feel like I have the weight of the world on my shoulders. I'm not like you Sammy. The only expectations you have are the ones you put on yourself. I not only have the ones I put on myself but the one's that the firm puts on me and now that Ness has passed on they've been doubled, then there's the expectations of you and Syl and the expectation that I have the wherewithal to start and open my own brokerage firm and then last but certainly not least there's the fact that I'm having an affair with my assistant and how I tell my wife who I love dearly but no longer choose to be with that it's over?"

Sammy could feel the elation over this revelation growing strong within her and could a smile blossoming until she glanced at his face which arched in anguish at the mere thought of telling Syl that the marriage she had worked so long and hard at was over.

"Oh, baby," Sammy, said feeling Anthony's pain as she pulled his head to her bosom. "Don't you think you're being a bit too hasty? You know and even though it might seem that I would be the first person to celebrate you leaving your wife it just doesn't make good business sense at this point in time. I mean you are the centerpiece, the calling card, the main attraction when it comes to attracting investors and how does it look when you're going through a domestic crisis and can't handle or keep your own house in order when you want them to entrust you with handling their investments and life savings? That would be totally contrary to what you're trying to establish."

Samantha eased up off the loveseat and made her way to the tiny bar and poured two healthy glasses of Patron. Handing one to Anthony she glanced at this pillar of a man she was so attracted to turning to grains of salt as he wallowed in his own pity.

"I hear you Sammy and you're absolutely right but I can't continue with this charade."

"What charade is that?"

"This so-called marriage. It's bullshit. It's been over a year since I can honestly say that I have felt anything closely resembling what we shared this past week. There's no spontaneity, no passion, and the closest thing I feel when it comes to love is that same type of love you feel for a pet or a sibling. Do you feel me? But I don't know for a woman it's different. There's no doubt that Syl loves me to death. I'd bet my life on that. Problem is I just don't feel the same anymore."

"With every relationship there is always an ebb and flow. There are always the ups and downs. And neither person is going to be at the same point when it comes to the strength of their emotions. But that's the beauty of marriage. You make a pact for better or worse and though it's beautiful in the beginning everyone knows though that a marriage is work and wrought with pitfalls but your love and commitment says that you will work through whatever. And even when you're feeling like this you have to go back to the trenches and examine on those things that made you make that commitment in the first place."

"You certainly seem to know a lot about something you have yet to experience."

"It's always been my belief that you don't necessarily have to fall in a shithole to know there's shit there. And I don't have to be married to know all the intricacies of what makes and breaks a marriage."

"Touche."

"But in your case, and this is really biting my nose to spite my face but you have to hang in there for a while and at least until the deal goes through and you're up and running if you're really serious about doing the damn thing. The real question is are you?"

"Hell yeah. How can you even ask me that? As arrogant as I am how long do you think I can bite my tongue while Mitchell & Ness routinely promise and pimp me at the same time? C'mon Sammy. Act like you know."

"I know but you need to reaffirm your focus from time-to-time and prioritize shit accordingly. Ain't no way a strong Black man like you going to let a female jeopardize what you've worked so long and hard for. I don't care if she is your wife. How do they say it? Money over bitches baby. In this world it's every man for himself. And if it means stringing Syl along for a cool mil then give her some catnip and a ball of yarn and string the bitch along."

"I hear you," Ant said dropping his head to hide the tears, "but I just can't do that. Syl's been everything and more than a man can ask for the past twelve years."

"Okay, and your point is?"

"I just can't walk in and say something off the cuff like sorry babe I'm tired of your old ass and tired of this marriage and I think it's time I bounce. You be cool and drive slow homey. How the fuck does that sound?"

Samantha laughed. "Don't be so crass sweetie. No one's expecting you to do that and if you were so concerned with Syl's feelings and the state of your marriage you wouldn't have been up in the Radisson with me. What? Are you suddenly having an epiphany of sorts? Or is this just a latent reaction to the fact that you had a taste of the good good and where you have always been able to hit it and quit it you met your match this time and there just ain't no going back. Fact of the matter is you fell, hook line and sinker and well it's just like being in quicksand. The more you wriggle the deeper you sink."

"Could be," Anthony said smiling, "but the fact still remains that I have a situation and there's no easy way out. And because I have a change of heart the fact remains that I did take a vow for better or worse and I owe her. I mean I made a commitment."

"You're right but first and foremost you should be committed to your own happiness and that doesn't mean staying in a bad situation and suffering just because. Still, timing is essential. Start the firm. Get it up and running. Gain your investors confidence. After all, stocks are all a confidence game. Make them believe that you are the closest thing there is to a financial savior and when you have them firmly in your grasp then and only then can you begin worrying about the course of your marriage. In the meantime, play the role. Be good to her. Love her. Put some money away for her and when you do decide to let her down, let her down easy and with a comfort level that will take the very venom from her fangs. Make her love you even as you depart. You know be a typical man instead of a man with some semblance of a conscious and don't worry about me Ant. I'll be here waiting in the wings as I have for the last seven years. Another year or so won't kill me. At least I know where your heart lies now."

"You'd wait for me Sammy?"

"I've waited this long. Why would things change now? This is the closest I've ever been lover. It took some time for you to wake up and smell the coffee but damn if you don't know the difference between that generic shit you've been sipping and this full-bodied deep, hearty, robust blend of a woman now in your midst," she laughed.

Anthony laughed before grabbing her glass and putting it on the mahogany end table and taking her in his arms and kissing her deeply.

"Stop baby," Sammy said pushing him away. "Now what I want you to do is go home and spend the weekend with your wife. Think of the days when there was nothing better than rushing home to Syl's arms. Even if you're not feeling it make yourself believe it. I know you're not feeling it but there are a lot of people that need you to be the Denzel of the Dow Jones, the Wesley of Wall Street. Syl ain't no slouch so you're going to have to put on an Academy Award winning performance to make her believe that you're more in love with her than you've ever been because whether you realize it or not she can wreck more havoc than any competitor or potential threat on the horizon. You know what they say. Ain't no wrath like a woman scorned. "

"You right."

"A woman always is. You see O'Bama in the presidency, but truth be told if Michelle runs Barack then who really runs the country? Think about it. Now much as I hate to say it go home and do the damn thang."

"I just know you're not putting me out," Anthony smiled almost incredulously.

"No, I'm not putting you out love; just putting you on pause. And like I said if I waited this long for you then I'm just going to have to wait a little longer to have what I truly want and that's a man without conflict. When you come to me next time I want you to come of your own free-will, of your own volition, free of worry and guilt."

"And how do you know I won't have a change of heart?"

Samantha sat for a moment.

"Because I have the security of knowing that there are very few women out there that have what I have to offer and now that you've had a chance to drink from the well of my generosity and love it'll be hard to look away."

"That confident, huh?"

"Wouldn't exactly say that but I am hoping that these few days we spent together will fill you with the memories that won't have you do anything but resign yourself to the fact that there can be no one else but Sammy," she said smiling as she grabbed his hat and jacket, handed them to him and pushed him to the door.

"I think I love you," were the last words Anthony said before the young woman closed the door.

'I hope you do and I hope you love me enough to bring you back', Sammy thought as a tear rolled from her eye as she leaned on the now closed door.

* *

"Damn Anthony! Where have you been," Sylvia shouted, a smile a mile wide on her face as he entered the front door of the fine brick home. "I went through all the trouble of fixing your favorite meal and timing it just so it would be piping hot when my baby walked through the door. You're usually home at six forty-five and if you're going to be late you usually call and let me know. But no call, no nothing and now your dinner's cold."

"Sorry baby."

"Sorry? You know it's never the same when it's reheated and you know how you hate me using the microwave to reheat anything," Syl said not even bother to glance in his direction so caught up in her labors. "And where's my kiss?" she said pursing her lips to receive her usual after work kiss that he'd use to rush home to. "You know I go to see momma for a week and come back and it's almost like we're strangers. I don't know what's happened in the time I was gone but if I didn't know my baby better I'd think he was having an affair," she laughed knowing full well the way she put it down and took care of her baby that that was the least of her worries. Besides any man holding two full time jobs hardly had time to have an affair. And as demanding and high maintenance as she knew she was along with Ant's determination to stay at the top there was no way he could possibly do anything besides rest when it was all said and done.

Breaking the Mancini's Italian bread in two before putting the rest of the loaf away Syl looked at Ant whose expression had hardly changed despite her attempts at humor.

"Whoa! What's wrong? Did my baby have an exceptionally trying day?"

"Something like that," he muttered.

"No worries, baby. Mommy's here to relieve any stress," Syl said forcing him into the chair at the dining room table. "Just you sit back and let mommy take care of her sweetie pie," Syl said before taking the briefcase Anthony still clutched. "Unbutton your shirt, love."

Doing as he was told Anthony unbuttoned the shirt.

"Now lift your arms up."

Again he did as he was told and much as he did not want Sylvia to touch him he thought of Sammy's words and followed her lead. Bare now from the waist up he was just glad that her relieving his needs— whatever that meant—hadn't involved him removing his trousers. He wasn't in the mood for Syl; didn't know if he ever would be again and certainly didn't want her touching him or trying to make love to him. He had long ago come to the conclusion that intercourse without love was simply cold sex and those days had long since passed.

Syl walked to the kitchen as Anthony watched. In her pale blue lounge outfit there wasn't an ounce of fat and Syl was as always as shapely and beautiful as she'd ever been but no longer did she stir him. What was it that daddy was so fond of saying. 'Familiarity breeds contempt.'

Moments later she returned with a salad and the main entrée. Veal parmesan had always been his favorite dish and although not always easy to find she had made it a point early in the marriage to teach her the fine art of making it to please her man. Now once or twice a year she prepared it and he had to admit he had never tasted better. It was an all-day process and she would usually get up early and begin the process making sure she let the sauce and ingredients blend and marinade thee greater portion of the day. The smell of it would drive Anthony insane and the anticipation would often times make him leave home on the days she was preparing it for him. He loved it but the veal would always be a backdrop for some earth shattering news and Anthony expected as much but was hardly in the mood for it tonight. Despite all the things Sammy had said to him just minutes earlier he could not bring himself to feel this woman now in his presence. And although he knew Syl had not changed he could not bring himself to acknowledge her or her efforts on this night.

"Baby, do me a favor and just relax. Let mommy take care of you and trust me if it's work stressing you think of it as only a temporary situation," she said smiling.

Anthony did his best to smile and go along with her as she placed the steaming hot platter in front of him. Looking at her as she chattered away his mind wandered as she chattered away about this and that. Her love apparent, Syl seemed genuinely happy, happier than he'd ever seen her and he couldn't imagine what had her glowing but whatever it was big and so he played the only role he could and quietly observed although the thought of Sammy continually clouded his thoughts and then suddenly he saw himself standing there in the doorway of her apartment whispering those words as an admission. He loved her. Over the years he'd come to appreciate her undying devotion and loyalty but in the past week it had transposed itself and he had to admit that there was something more and whatever it was he had to come to admit that he loved her. Maybe he'd always loved her despite his efforts to maintain a decorum of professionalism.

Syl was still chattering away.

"Anthony Pendleton! You haven't heard a word I've said."

"Huh?"

"Anthony where are you. You seem a thousand miles away. Are you alright baby?"

"Yeah, yeah. I'm fine baby. Just a little distracted is all."

"Distracted? You haven't even said anything about the veal after I spent all day preparing it for you. What the hell is so all consuming that you can't feel your loving wife's soothing hands giving her baby a back massage and the dinner she's taken all this time preparing for you," Syl said now putting her concerns on the backburner and focusing on Anthony. "You've always had the ability to separate work from your marriage so whatever it is it's really bothering you. Tell me something. What happened while I was away? I threw out the fact that you didn't even bother to call me the whole time I was gone rationalizing it and saying that you needed some time away from my nagging. Thought maybe you needed some me time and so I didn't bother you. Figured that that was only natural for a couple that's been married for over a decade. I tried to give you your space. And then I said you may even be trying to work on trying to set everything in place for opening your firm and I even felt a little guilty about all the pressure I'd put on you before I left and so I made it a point to leave you alone and let you enjoy life without me if that's possible," she said laughing at her own attempts at lightening the mood. "But it seems that under the current circumstances that neither of those was the right approach seeing you tonight. You know this is the first night we've really had a chance to spend together since I've been gone and you're as distant as I've ever seen you," she said filling his glass for what seemed like the fourth or fifth time with the rather light Zinfadel before going back to massaging his back and shoulders.

"So, tell me Ant. What the fuck is going on."

Again he thought of Sammy's words and managed to mutter. "Nothing baby. I'm okay."

"You are not okay Anthony. After twelve years you don't think I know my husband? I was joking before but all jokes aside tell me honestly. Are you having an affair?"

Anthony thought but was smart enough to know that taking too much time in responding would only arouse further suspicion and hastily answered a resounding 'no'.

"I hope not. You know my history and if that were to happen it would probably kill me and especially at this point."

"What point is that?"

"Do you want some more wine sweetheart?"

"Now you have me wondering? What's up Syl? If I didn't know you better I'd think you were trying to get me drunk."

Syl smiled.

"I have some great news baby and then I have something that may be a little disturbing but let me you the good news first."

"I'm listening," Ant said pouring himself another glass of wine in preparation for the news. The day had been a roller coaster ride of emotions and he wasn't sure if he could stand another upheaval of any sort.

"Go ahead."

"Well sweetie when I was in North Carolina I did a little fundraising on your behalf. I called in a few old friends and my markers and was able to raise close to two million on your behalf. I would have told you sooner but I wanted to wait until I had the money in hand and it was confirmed before I said anything."

"You did what?" Anthony said the smile flooding his dark brown face.

"I thought might bring you around and take whatever's on your mind off. If I followed my premonitions I'd have to say that it's either another woman or the pressure of opening the firm that has you out of sorts. And being that I know how much you love me and that there's not another woman on God's green earth that could love you as much as I do I would have to say that it's the pressure of raising the start- up monies in such a short amount of time that has you down. I knew that when I went away and my premonitions are right that's what has you down. Am I right?"

Anthony was so elated at the news that all he could was rise up, take Syl in his arms and lift her tiny brown frame off the floor.

"I love you baby," he said whispering in her ear as she tore at the buttons of his shirt. Ripping the buttons off and wrapping her legs around him he felt her hands tugging at his belt buckle and then unbuckling his pants. Before they'd hit the floor he was entering her slowly at first and then with all the unbridled passion of a man hell bent on erasing all the guilt and demons from his very soul.

"Easy baby," she whispered but he was of no mind to hear her as he drove the length of his manhood deeper with each thrust. He loved her of this he was sure. He appreciated her but he hated the fact that she had given her very heart and soul to him making him responsible to her and she responsible to and for him when all he wanted to do was be alone and regain his life.

Driving deeper he felt the tears roll down his face as he drove himself up in her again and again as she screamed now of joy but out of pain and for the first time since that dreadful experience in college she felt as if she didn't know this man who now lay atop of her.

"You're hurting me Anthony,' she cried out her words resonating throughout the modest brick home. But her words fell on deaf ears and for the second time in her life she felt she was no more than a body to be used and the way only a rape victim could feel. This man who claimed to be her husband, this same man who claimed he loved her had defiled her as no other man had and she couldn't understand it. When it was over she left it alone and thought of all the times he'd expressed his love in the bedroom and decided to let it go. His eyes still welled with tears when it was all over and she still was having problems comprehending but dared not to speak of it again and when he Kingd off of her he seemed as cold and distant as he'd been before she'd broken the news. Something was wrong although Sylvia had no idea what. She had two theories and expressed as much and though he'd barely commented he had admitted that the stress was taking control of him. Or had he? He certainly hadn't conceded to having an affair which was the only possible alternative for his sudden change in behavior but then why would he and if truth be told she had hardly allowed or given him the opportunity to admit anything so busy was she touting her own attributes. And then she'd led with the story of how she'd done fundraising in the amount of close to two million and any man no matter what the issue would hardly rock the boat in lieu of that much cold cash. Still, she'd been through more than anything Anthony could ever bestow on her and if it was one thing Sylvia truly believed it was that a man despite all his attributes could never outwit, out think, or out maneuver a woman and especially as one so experienced and so well-endowed at the game as she. And though he was her husband and she loved him she would not, could not allow a man, any man to break her and leave her destitute and broken. No something was amiss with Anthony though she couldn't rightly put her finger on it. Something had transpired while she'd been away and even though she couldn't pinpoint it at present one thing was for sure. She would. But before she would do that there was one more thing she had to say to him. A litmus test for sure there were two things she had to confront him with and if this didn't elicit a response nothing would and so as she made her way to the bathroom she gathered her thoughts. Sitting on the toilet letting the water run til it was nice and hot she took the washrag down and placed it in the sink to warm it before heading to the living room and pouring two healthy shots of Patron. More like doubles she made her way back to the bedroom and handed one to Anthony who lay there staring at some old black and white movie on the tube.

"Thank you," he muttered meekly as she handed him the glass and returned to the bathroom. The sink was almost completely full and she thanked her lucky stars that it hadn't overflowed. Another minute, she thought and only prayed as she applied the warm compress to her vagina that Anthony wasn't going to be another spill on her already soiled life.

Entering the boudoir once more he appeared in much better spirits and she attributed to his empty glass on the nightstand.

"Come here baby," he said reaching for her. Syl in no mood for another tryst her pussy still throbbing moved gingerly towards him. Always there for her man she had in all their years together never denied him but if ever there were a time this would have been the time.

"Promise me that you'll be gentle," was all she could mutter.

"And what's that supposed to mean?"

"Well, a few minutes ago I thought you were digging for gold. You hurt me Anthony and I tried to tell you you were hurting me and you just ignored and kept on plugging away like I wasn't even there."

"Sorry, baby. Guess I just got lost in your love."

"Lost in my love. Is that what you call it? Felt more like you were just fucking some common street ho."

"Oh, damn. I'm sorry if I came across that way. Come here and let me make it up to you," he grinned grabbing her by the waist.

"Anthony?"

"Yeah, baby," he said pulling her on top of him.

Straddling him now she eased down on him emitting a gasp as he entered her. She rode him slowly at first and then increased her speed as she felt him well up inside of her. She could him expand as the walls of her vagina stretched to encompass the man inside of her. They were moving in unison now and she loved this.

"Anthony."

"Yes, sweetheart."

"Baby?"

"Talk to me."

"There's something I need to say to you."

"What is it sweetheart?"

"Baby, I'm pregnant."

With this concession it felt like the weight of the world had finally been lifted and with each word Syl gasped flooding him. When it was over she looked down only to find Anthony staring at her as if he'd just witnessed something cataclysmic.

"Did you hear me?" she said as she headed to the bathroom and grabbed a towel. Wiping herself off she handed the towel to him to do the same.

"You okay," she said smiling only hoping that he felt the same joy she did at that moment but there was no reply.

"See, that's why I was afraid to tell you. I wasn't sure how you would respond. I know we've talked about it in the past but sweetheart I'm damn near forty and the only thing I haven't given you is a child and I wanted to—I guess I wanted to for selfish reasons—have your baby."

Still, unable to respond Anthony held out his arms. Stunned by this latest revelation he tears flowed freely. It was the second time he'd shed tears today and he truly wondered if he were having a nervous breakdown. He wondered if God was punishing him for his indiscretions. After professing his love for Samantha and all but telling her she was the reason for his leaving Syl she'd all but told him to man up and stop with the whining and go home to his wife and when he'd taken her advice and gotten home to his wife who he hardly loved and could hardly stand the sight of anymore despite her obvious beauty he was shocked to find that she was pregnant after twelve years of marriage. And what made it all the worse he was on the brink of leaving her and embarking on a new career. And now here she stood with a cool two million and a child to boot. The life that had seemed all so simple only a week before was now complicated and confusing. His mind a myriad of images he wept quietly as he held her tightly in his arms and tried to make sense of it all while all the time whispering I love you in her ear.

Syl sensing that all was good was relieved to know that her Ant loved after all and despite whatever it was that was causing him through so much heartache and pain fell asleep in the comfort of the arms of her lover, her friend and her husband.

And life went on its usual course for some time afterwards. Syl was never happier calling mommy every day, sometimes three and four times a day. Anthony seemed happy as well and the plans for the firm went on as planned. Assuming the partnership at Mitchell and Ness he was now afforded the necessary revenues even without Syl's contributions and Sammy assumed her position as his assistant as though their little liaison had never happened. Life for Anthony was now everything he could ever hope for but those who knew him and watched him closely knew that there was still deeply troubling him.

Chapter5

"How are things going at home?" Sammy inquired one day just to make sure that they were still on the same page.

"All's well on the Western Front," he replied smiling not wanting to go into detail or the fact that Syl was pregnant and raise any guilt or suspicion in Sammy's eyes.

The only real or obvious difference was the number of people who entered the office each day to meet with Mr. Pendleton. Businessmen with dapper blue and black suits paraded in and out since Anthony had become one of the chief executive officers at Mitchell and Ness and Anthony seemingly held and welcomed the position as if he had done so all his life.

Samantha kept the office atmosphere light and cordial and afforded all of Mr. Pendleton's visitor's the professional courtesy one could possibly be offered and they appreciated it and often returned it afforded Samantha everything from tickets to Knick games to theatre tickets. That was the world of Wall Street, the constant bartering for favors, which in turn could mean a meeting with Mr. Pendleton when there was virtually no room on his schedule for weeks. And everyone knew that Samantha virtually ran the offices of Mitchell and Ness alone so she was the person you had to be in with if you wanted to have any maneuverability within the firm. They all did this and were pretty much on a first name basis with Sammy. That was all but one. A tall, handsome, well-dressed gentleman of between thirty-five and forty of Italian descent known only as Mr. Assante began frequenting the offices of Mitchell and Ness not long after Anthony Pendleton gained his promotion. He intrigued Samantha though not in a romantic sense but only because of all the men who made their way into his office he stood out. Always nattily attired he reminded Samantha not of the typical Wall Street broker types in their drab navy blue or charcoal gray Brooks bros. Suits with the traditional tan London Fog trench coats but more like a Mafia don with his pinstriped doubled breasted suits and striped shirts with pastel colored ties often bordering on taking a fashion risk but for the most part he was well dressed and anyone looking could tell his suits were tailored made and expensive. Still, after being in the Wall

Street area for close to a decade it was easy to notice when someone didn't fit with the normal entourage and although he was polite and manner able there was something about Mr. Assante that bothered Samantha. He'd meet with Anthony on the average of once every two weeks and each time he entered the office and despite the flowers he'd bring Sammy each time he stopped through she made her uneasy. She had a hard time seeing the connection between he and Anthony and although nowhere in her job description was she designated his bodyguard she felt it her duty to watch out for his welfare. And since Anthony was mum when it came to the topic of Mr. Assante Samantha made it a point on this particular afternoon to take the rather well- heeled young man into an adjoining office and question him about his relationship with Anthony.

"Come in Mr. Assante. Mr. Pendleton had some rather unexpected business he had to take care of. He may be gone the better part of an hour. Is there anything that I may be able to help you with?"

"I wish there were Samantha but I'm afraid Mr. Pendleton's affairs are rather confidential so to answer your questions I would have to say no."

"Again are you sure there's nothing I can do to be of service to you?"

The young man smiled.

"I'm afraid not unless you decide to have dinner with me tonight."

"I wish I could but I'm afraid my husband wouldn't approve."

"I'm quite sure he wouldn't mind being that you're not married. Although I admit it's a good line."

"Don't assume Mr. Assante..."

"In my line of work one can never assume Samantha. All we can do is our homework, leaving no stone unturned. False assumptions can all too often prove fatal. Our science has got to be factual and exact. The slightest error in detail can mean life and death."

"Sounds rather frightening."

"It can be at times," Mr. Assante replied. There was no smile on his face now and Sammy now realizing that she may have bitten off more than she could chew was quickly looking for a way out. The man was dangerous with a cold steel look in his eyes devoid of any emotion and she quickly realized that he would just as soon slice her neck as to kiss her. "Do you have any more questions Samantha," he asked fixing the smile right back on his face.

Sammy was frightened now but still wondered.

"Just one Mr. Assante. What is it that you do and what is the affiliation with Mr. Pendleton."

"As I said before Samantha, my affiliations with Mr. Pendleton are strictly confidential. All I can tell you is that I am in Mr. Pendleton's employ and my client's interests are strictly my clients so if he wishes to divulge the nature of our business he is fully in his right to do so. However, I am not at liberty to discuss the nature of our business. Now may I ask you something?"

"Certainly."

"Why are you so concerned with the nature of Mr. Pendleton's personal affairs?"

"Well, to be honest with you most of the goings on of Mitchell and Ness I am privy to but your name does not show up in any of our records or files and yet you meet with every two weeks as though you are discussing your portfolio. You know as if it's Mitchell and Ness business."

"And I guess in a way it is," he laughed. "Now if you'll excuse me I must be going. I have another meeting uptown in about an hour. Will you tell Anthony I'm sorry I missed him and tell him I'll be in touch."

"I'll do that."

"I know you will and that dinner invitation remains open."

"I'll remember that."

Less than an hour later Anthony walked in and though there were people in the lobby waiting to see him Samantha made it a point to speak to him first. She was quite adamant in her approach and Anthony had to admit that he had never seen Samatha quite so animated.

"Mr. Assante just left."

"Oh, that's right. I completely forgot his appointment. Did he leave a message?"

"A message? The man wouldn't talk to me. Every time I'd asked him a question he'd tell me he couldn't reveal anything because it was confidential and that I should ask you if I have any questions."

"Okay and what's the problem?" He said shuffling some papers and looking for something on his desk.

"The problem is I don't like him. I don't like anything about him. Call it women's intuition or whatever. I don't know. All I know is there's something wrong with him. He just seems sheisty to me. I don't know if he's a gangster or if he's connected but there's something that strikes me as being shady."

"Don't concern yourself with Mr. Asssante. I'll take care of him now who's waiting to see me?"

Samantha stared at Anthony in disbelief.

Anthony walked Samantha through the office lobby nodding to the receptionist and doormen as he did so. He was glad to have Sammy in his corner but at this point he hardly needed her worrying about him. It just added to his own worries and there was little she could do at this point. The ball was in his court and it was time for him to simply man up. There was a rough road ahead full of tough decisions and it was up to him to work his way through them. Not for a minute had he ever doubted his capabilities but this was another league altogether. Go Fish had turned into high stakes poker and he knew it was crunch time and no time to fold.

Samantha was chattering away about something but he hardly heard. It was starting to drizzle.

"You need a ride Sammy?"

"Never thought you'd ask," she replied as Anthony grabbed her arm and pulled under the umbrella and out of the rain.

"Come on. My car's just down the block in the garage. Reaching the car Anthony hit the remote and held the door open for the young woman and watched as she pulled her perfectly tapered olive legs so narrow at the ankles into the car. He immediately felt his nature rise and at any other time he would have paid attention to the desire welling up inside of him but sex had become ancient history in lieu of Syl's pregnancy and he couldn't remember the last time he had taken a break to even indulge. Syl's pregnancy and the thought of it did even more to leave a bad taste in his mouth and make him shy away but the smell of Sammy's perfume and the sight of those shapely legs brought back the fond memories of the week they had spent together. Shuffling through his pants pockets Anthony found the car keys and started to insert them into the ignition when there was a loud crash and the sound of glass shattering interrupted the silence. Anthony's trance was immediately broken as Samantha screamed. Two men stood on either side of the late model BMW guns drawn.

Anthony at first shocked by the sudden intrusion remained calm despite what seemed to be a life-threatening situation.

"Get the fuck out the car nigga," the young Black man on the passenger side said grabbing Samantha and dragging her out of the car. Samantha continued screaming.

"Shut the hell up bitch! Now you have a choice. We can do this peacefully or we can do this the uptown way and can take your pretty White ass someplace it ain't never been before," he said smiling before drawing back the butt of the nine meter he clutched in his hand and letting go with all he could muster and knocking Samantha back on her ass. She was quiet now stunned by the sudden assault that had her dizzy and her head spinning.

Despite it all Ant remained calmed and focused on the man who stood before him. No stranger to street violence had never grown accustomed to it but was certainly used to it. And he knew the desperation that drew men to do things in the streets. He also knew that there were two kinds of gangstas. There were the ones that loved the thrill of taking down a score and then there were the ones that felt the pressure or the need of pulling off a score. Whether it bit or the need to eat these were the more dangerous of the two it was obvious that the man who held the gun to his head was the latter. Nose dripping and shaking gently it was apparent that he hadn't had his medicine for the day and his jones had the better of him. It would be hours before he could unload the car and the thought itself made him angry.

"Come on man. Get out of the car and give me your wallet. And hurry it the fuck up. I ain't got no time for you fake ass Uncle Tom niggas. I'd just as soon bust a cap in your ass as not. Now hurry the fuck up nigga."

Anthony got out slowly seeing that the man was on edge and any sudden movement may have caused him to squeeze the trigger.

"Okay pardner. Anything you say. You be easy now ya hear. I'm just reaching in my pocket to get my wallet as you requested."

Handing him the wallet Anthony noticed entering the garage and just as suddenly as it appeared it was gone. Anthony looked to see how Samantha was faring and could see the fear in her eyes.

"It's going to be okay baby," he said managing a smile in hopes that it would somehow comfort her.

"Okay gentlemen, you have my money and the keys to the car so if you don't mind do you mind if we leave now?"

"Shut the fuck up nigga. You ain't runnin' shit here."

Unfazed by the nine the man held on him, Anthony walked around the car to where Samantha still sat on the ground.

"You okay baby?" He asked his concern showing. Looking up she nodded briefly before something caught her eye. The second hi-jacker oblivious to the goings on rummaged through her purse searching for her purse.

"Get what ya getting Tre and let's get out of here," the older man now drenched in his own sweat cautioned.

"What's your rush?" a voice said as the two men turned quickly and into the face of a sawed off shotgun.

"Now if you want to be around to see another minute of daylight I suggest you put the pieces on the ground real nice and gentle like."

Stunned, the two men kneeled and placed the revolvers they held down and stood awaiting their sentences. Give them back their belongings and if you ever believed in Jesus or Allah I suggest you acknowledge Him now."

"Honest man we wasn't gonna hurt 'em. All we wanted was the car."

"That's hard for me to believe looking at the size of the shiner on that young ladies face," the man replied with little or no emotion showing. Any man who had ever been in the game knew that he was a man to be reckoned with, a man not to be toyed with, a man who could kill with little or no apprehension.

"Honest mister we didn't mean to hurt nobody," the younger man pleaded.

The tall White gentleman holding the sawed off shotgun ignored the remarks and instead turned his attention to Anthony.

"It's your car they were trying to steal so I'll let you make the call boss. You just let me know. You want me to send them back to the heavenly Father just say the word."

"No", Anthony managed to get out. "I think these boys have learned their lesson," he said smiling as he stared at the younger man's now wet trousers.

"You best be glad this here is a Christian man. Me, myself I would have blown your asses away and thought nothing of it. Would have been like taking the garbage out to me. You feel me?"

Both men nodded.

"Now get the fuck out of here," he said concealing the shotgun on the inside of his long, black, leather, trench coat.

"You okay Anthony?"

"Yeah, I'm good. You okay Samantha?"

"What can I say? I'm alive. I have never been so scared in all my life."

"It was a little nerve-wracking," Anthony said now seemingly a little more shaken than he was during the encounter. "I'm just glad you showed up when you did Joe. How the hell did you just happen along?"

"Well, I missed you last week and I didn't want to miss you again this week so I asked that cute little file clerk."

"Mindy," Samantha chimed in.

"Yeah, that's her name. Cute little thing. Is she married?"

"I don't think so," Anthony replied, "but anyway you were saying."

"Oh, she told me that you'd just left and if I hurried I could probably catch you but I didn't see you and was headed home. You just so happened in the only garage that I am and I was sorta on my guard because those two looked like they were up to no good when I parked so I guess I was sorta n my p's and q's when I got here and now I'm glad that I was."

"You certainly handled yourself well," Samantha added.

"Tricks of the trade. I grew up not far from here in Bensonhurst. When I was growing up that was an everyday occurrence. Only difference today is on what side of the gun you're on," he smiled. "Tony knows what I'm talking about. Uptown was the same way."

"No doubt," Anthony replied in agreement.

"But on the serious side I think you'd best be making headwinds. Those two are sure to return looking for someone else to jack. I don't know if you noticed how bad my man was shaking, nose running and junkies do some stupid shit when they need that shit."

"You're right," Anthony said pulling the tall Italian close and hugging him as old friends often do.

"Thanks again Joe."

"Not a problem. Just glad to be of help. You know I'm always down for you Tone. Always have been always will be."

"Listen I'll call you when I get settled."

"All right then. You two have a pleasant evening."

"Thank you, Mr. Assante," Samantha said as Anthony held the door for her.

"Call me Joe."

"Okay. Well thank you Joe," Samantha said gratefully.

Once inside and pulling out onto the busy street Anthony turned to the woman at his side.

"You okay Sammy?"

"I'm a little shaken but nothing a double of Patron won't cure," she replied doing her best to smile.

What bothered her more than the actual incident was that the assailants were Black. Damn all her life she had tried to erase the stereotype that ran so deeply about Black folks being lazy, drug users on welfare and criminals. Her parents had fought the same fight trying to teach her differently and rectify the ignorance that surrounded her. And she had actively fought it befriending anyone and everyone she came into contact with regardless of race or religion. But it had been an almost useless battle trying to reason with those with a limited scope of the world. She been dubbed everything from a liberal to a nigga lover but had stood her ground. She'd even gone so far as to convince herself that the world was wrong, (at least her world), when she'd met Anthony. He was the brightest star on Wall Street, a world shaker with the largest and most prestigious firm and he dispelled all their myths and stereotypes with his Blackness. She sometimes wished those bigots from Short Hills and Livingston could see him in the world of million dollar investments and see just how he commanded things. But now she felt hurt and violated almost as if she'd been wrong and those that had proclaimed Blacks criminals right. Looking at Anthony she knew she was wrong for thinking this way and yet the thought had surfaced and recurred several times not only during the attempted robbery but even now.

"Does that mean you'd like to stop for a drink? Heard they just opened a new Commuter's Café."

"After the day I've had all I want to do is get home to the comforts of my own little bed."

"Sorry I thought I heard you mention the fact that after the day you had you could stand a strong drink."

"You are not mistaken Mr. Pendleton and that's exactly what I plan on doing from the comforts of my own little bed."

They both laughed and it was obvious that the day had taken its toll on the woman. Pulling up in front of her building Anthony suddenly realized just how tired and fatigued he was as well.

"Have a nightcap with me?"

"The last time I was here you pushed me out the door and said I needed to go home to my wife and not come back 'til I had resolved that issue. Now you're asking me to come up and have a nightcap."

"You'd think after the day I just had you would be just a tad more comforting but I guess it's just common to your species that you have to be gruff and uncaring or you couldn't call yourself a man."

Ant laughed.

"Is that what I am? Gruff and uncaring?"

"As opposed to being gentle and caring? Yes, you are. Why can't you come in and sit for a few minutes and make sure that I am okay and sleeping peaceably before heading home to your beautiful Ebony princess?"

Anthony chuckled.

"You go ahead up while I find a parking space," he said smiling.

Anthony parked the car and headed to the apartment building.

"Ah, Mr. Pendleton it's been some time. Heard you got a big promotion? Congratulations!"

"Thanks Jimmy and it keeps me swamped. One of the reasons you haven't seen me and the reason I'm here this evening. That's all I do is work. I'm here tonight to tie up some loose ends," he lied.

"I guess that's why you get the big bucks."

"Big bucks? You obviously know something that I don't know," he laughed.

Approaching the apartment, Anthony felt a certain uneasiness. Home on time every night like clockwork for the past three months Anthony was playing the role just as Sammy had suggested but his hatred had mellowed somewhat and Syl's infectious attitude and enthusiasm when it came to planning for the new baby had infected him as well. He had no intentions of going through with the charade but not knowing anything other than work and home he had fallen begrudgingly fallen into the routine. Now here he was at Sammy's and he knew one evening with her would have him morose and longing for something he simply couldn't have at this point in time. He thought to turn and walk right back to the car and go home but he deserved some happy in his life despite the heartache it would bring tomorrow.

Knocking softly Anthony was speechless when she opened the door dressed in a sheer black gown that revealed all. Her dark brown nipples protruded firmly against the front of the gown and he immediately thought of Syl's sagging lifeless breasts.

"Well, come in silly. Don't just stand there like this is all new to you. Besides you're going to give me a complex if you just stand there staring. I know I've put on a few pounds but I was under the impression that you liked thick as opposed to thin. At least that's what you told me."

"You're right and damn if the few extra pounds doesn't become you Sammy."

"Glad you approve," she said handing him a glass. "Come on in and have a seat Ant. I need to unwind a bit," she said then I want to talk you about a few things."

"Nothing too deep I hope. That was a rather harrowing experience we shared today so nothing to deep. I need to give it a rest as well."

"Oh come on Ant. You haven't talked to me in close to three months and if that shit hadn't happened I seriously doubt that you would have even been here tonight so please chill and just let me air some shit out. Will you do that for me?"

"I'm gonna need another one of these then," Anthony said reaching for the bottle of Patron.

"You just might," she replied before pouring herself another two fingered shot as well.

The Patron warmed his insides and it wasn't long before he began to stretch out on the plush burgundy loveseat.

"Go ahead love. Tell me what's on your mind."

"I will but first I want you to do me a favor love."

"You name it," Anthony replied feeling the Patron.

"Come over here."

Anthony stood and proceeded to walk across the living room.

"Now bend down," she commanded before grabbing the back of his head and pulling him down to her. With her free hand she pulled the front of her gown down and held her breast up close to his face.

"Now kiss it," she purred pulling his head to her nipple. As he did what she said Sammy relaxed sighing deeply before pulling it away just as quickly as she'd given it to him.

"Tell me you want me Anthony."

"You know I do Sammy."

"Then why has it been so long?"

Anthony stood now and stared at the attractive young woman before him.

"Why are you staring at me?"

"I'm just trying to figure out if it's me or are all the woman I come into contact with traveling with only a half a load."

"And what's that mean."

"Well, let me see if I can put this in perspective or better yet in turns that you might understand. If a man tells you to leave him alone what are you going to do?"

"Guess I'm going to leave him alone."

"Exactly and did you not tell me to back away and bide my time?"

"Yes, those were my words but I also told you that I was in love with you and I believe you said the same. And that's not what two people in love do. They find ways to talk, to hold each other, to love each other. At least that's my understanding. What they don't do is act like strangers. Now come here and hold me. Show me that you love me."

It was at that moment that Anthony knew he wanted Sammy more than anything he'd ever wanted in his life. Taking her in his arms he lost count of how many times they made love that night before he passed out. But it wasn't long before he felt the softness of her lips on his back. Stirring slightly he heard her sultry voice whispering to him.

"I was tempted to let you sleep through the night baby but I think you need to get up but that would just be selfish. I'm sure Syl is worried sick."

Sore and unable to respond Anthony sat up and took one of Sammy's cigarettes.

"Thought there was something you wanted to talk to me about."

"It can wait."

"You got my curiosity up. Talk to me Sammy."

There was a long pause. Sammy took the cigarette from Anthony's hand and poured herself another shot of Patron before turning the night light on and staring into Anthony's eyes.

"Anthony I need you to be honest with me. I want you to be totally and brutally honest about something."

"I'm listening."

"Well, some people consider me attractive. And a lot of the brothers look at me as no more than a hot White chick—you know like unchartered waters—like another conquest. Do you see me like that? Be honest with me."

Anthony took both the glass and cigarette from Sammy and smiled.

"There's no doubt about you being attractive. You are definitely a head turner, a stunner. My dad would call you a stallion. And I say that with the utmost respect and in the most complimentary of fashions. But I longed a long time ago that it's not what appears on the outside but what a person maintains within. Seven years ago, when you first came on board I was shook by your beauty but I was also very much in love with my wife. But over time I came to know you and appreciate you as a person. I admired your drive and your intelligence. I gravitated to you because of your loyalty and eventually and despite my marriage and my hang ups about race I fell in love with you. You know it's funny and don't get bent out of shape when I say this but I wanted a 320i for the longest time. I've always been in love with BMW's but I never wanted the seven series even though they're more luxurious and more prestigious. No I wanted a 320i. Now I know people look at me and say why is Anthony driving that when he can afford the top of the line and I hear them whispering but I don't give a fuck. The 320i is what appeals to me. Now there's a new girl at Mitchell & Ness. Kara something and all the brokers are head over heels in lust over her but ya know I sat down with her going over her responsibilities and although she is quite an attractive girl..."

"She is quite pretty," Samantha added.

"Yes, she is but after sitting with her for maybe a half an hour I came to the conclusion that she's half an idiot and that's the good half so you see the looks although appealing don't mean shit if you ain't got nothin' to accompany them. And as far as the brothers wanting a White girl as a trophy all I can say is you got the wrong brother. Like I said I have hang ups about race that it may take me a lifetime to work through but thanks to you I'm on it. Why do you ask?"

"Before I get to that point let me ask you this. Do you really love me?"

"I already think you know the answer to that."

"So, and with you professing your undying love and devotion to me and if Syl weren't in the picture would you marry me?"

Anthony was quiet. Why was it that every time he disclosed the fact that he had feelings for a woman the idea of marriage inevitably came up? Did they have a recessed gene that rose up every time sex became an issue? He wondered. This was not the first time the subject had come up after some good loving.

"Anthony, I asked you a question."

"So would I and do I love you enough to marry you? Is that what you're asking me?"

"That's it in the nutshell."

"There's no doubt in my mind that I love you enough to marry you but the question I have is the world ready for us to be married and would our love be strong enough to survive the shit the world would throw at us simply because we're from different worlds, from different cultures. I think that's the real question and the real hardship for me."

Samantha dropped her head and Anthony could see the tears drip from her face.

"Whoa! Whoa! Whoa! Why all the questions and the tears baby?" Anthony said sorry now that he hadn't just told her what she wanted to hear.

"Because the weight gain isn't just a sheer freak of nature Anthony. I'm pregnant with your child Anthony."

Anthony wondered if he were suffering from a relapse. Was it déjà vu or had she actually said she was pregnant? Still, with all his reservations he hardly felt the way he had when Syl told him the same thing just months earlier but here he was a married man well vested in his career with two children on the way by two different women and one wasn't his wife. Much as he hated the thought of being bound to Syl for the next thirty or forty years he knew that Syl was the logical choice and though she was near the end of her childbearing years and aging by the minute she was after all his wife. The fact that he didn't love her anymore was irrelevant in everyone's eyes but his own. And yet he knew that there would be nothing but congratulatory slaps on the back and things would continual as a matter of course with the news of her pregnancy.

Sammy's pregnancy on the other hand would cause a multitude of problems with everyone include his new partner, Mr. Mitchell who he was sure would frown on not just the idea of his infidelity but the fact that it was a White woman within the workplace and he knew as well as anyone that the firm had a strict policy when it came to staff fraternization for just this reason. His clients, who were predominantly White would also have a problem with the idea that this nigga who had the nerve to climb the corporate ladder to the unprecedented status of partner in one of the last bastions of White male supremacy had not only taken a position they deemed just a matter of time before he bit the dust but one of their women as well. And yet despite all of these factors and the apparent complications that came along with it Anthony felt a glow he had not known before. Turning to Samantha he hugged her tightly eliciting the joy he felt deep inside of him.

"I was so fearful of telling you this Ant. With all the stress and melodrama you're experiencing right through here I know it's neither the right time nor the right thing to do at this point."

Anthony laughed aloud.

"Let me tell you something my father told me a long time ago."

"What's that Ant?"

"My dad told me never to lie down with a woman unless you're ready to take care of that woman and the child she may get up with."

"That's very honorable and I admire that kind of courage and loyalty in a man but you and I both know how this will be looked upon at not only the firm but out in the world itself. I'm still not sure if we live in a society ready for an interracial couple and multiracial children."

"I feel you."

"I mean it would take its toll on us but what about the child. Is it fair to subject any child to to the cruelties that come along with growing up in a racist society?"

"It's something we'd have to really take a long look at Sammy. Let's say over dinner tomorrow night."

"Sounds good to me."

"Dinner it is then or better yet why don't we just make a weekend of it and hash things over. I've been meaning to meet with Boots on the Magi account. We could fly down to Baltimore after work tomorrow and grab a room right on the inner harbor and spend a little time together."

Sammy was ecstatic.

"Oh my God! Are you serious Ant? Let me just call mommy and let her know that I won't be able to go shopping and see what else I have to clear off my schedule and I'll let shoot you an e-mail by lunchtime to confirm."

"Sounds good. Now let me get out of here before Syl gets too suspicious."

"Alright," Sammy said grinning from ear-to-ear as she watched Ant walk to the front door.

"Sammy," he said turning to the scantily clad young woman staring adoringly at him.

"Yes, love."

"I want you to know that I am madly in love with you."

"Is that right?" she said patronizing.

"Madly."

"Then I've done my job," she giggled before pulling the covers over her head.

Locking the door and making his leave Anthony smiled briefly at the thought of the evening before turning his thoughts to the task before him. He hoped Syl was sound asleep and wouldn't meet him with a hundred questions as to why he hadn't bothered to call and his whereabouts.

Chapter 6

Arriving home an half an hour later he checked to make sure he hadn't worn Sammy's perfume home and to make sure he sprayed a rather liberal amount of Dolce and Gabbana he kept in the car for just this reason. Once inside, he poured himself a double of

Cuervo just to ease the tension and be prepared for the grilling he knew was about to be administered.

Syl appeared to be sleep and as was his habit he bent over her limp body and kissed her lightly on the cheek.

"You could have at least called Anthony. You know you had me worried to death."

"Sorry baby. I just got caught up and I guess the job is really starting to take its toll on me. I met with clients almost up to closing and the whole time Samantha's clamoring to meet with me so I decided to walk her to her car so she could get whatever it was off her chest. Well, she's parked in the garage a block away. You know the one I always park in when these two thugs roll up, guns drawn and tried to rob us and steal the car."

"Are you serious?"

"Dead."

"Is she okay?"

"Yeah, she's fine. And off duty cop just happened along and pulled his gun and frightened them off. Well, actually he held them at gunpoint and asked me if I wanted to press charges or not?"

"And you said."

"Listen I have enough going on and I didn't want to spend two or three hours down at the police precinct filing charges only so they could be freed before I got back to the office."

"So you allowed for them to go free so they could turn around and do the same thing to some other innocent people."

"I guess I did."

"Boy oh boy. My baby—the good Samaritan— whatever am I going to do with you. But now you can understand why I insist on you calling me when you're going to be late. There are crazy people out there Anthony. And with the economy as bad as it is people are liable to do anything these days."

"Don't you worry your pretty little head over me. I'm a big boy. I can take care of myself."

"Ain't never been worried over you Anthony. I'm worried about those other fools out there."

Anthony kissed her on the cheek again.

"You get some sleep now," he said pulling the cover up around her chin.

"You want me to put you to sleep baby?"

Anthony smiled.

"No, I'm good. You get some rest. I'll be fine. Oh, and by the way, I'm going to Baltimore this weekend to meet with Boots and try to close the account."

"You going to tell him you're planning on opening up your own firm?"

"I may mention it. Now go to sleep. You worry too much."

Syl smiled before closing her eyes.

Chapter7

Syl had been home for barely a week and Anthony had been late coming home three of those days. Not only that but he was different. Oh, sure there were the same little attempts at loving her but now they were empty ploys at hiding whatever it was he was trying to hide. At first she thought it was the added pressure of the new position but knowing this man as she did she knew it wouldn't be long before he had all his ducks in a row and had conquered the intricate details of his new position. No, there was more and as savvy and astute at the art of men and deception she hardly knew what was different. Sure he'd been coming in later but nine o'clock as opposed to seven was no big discrepancy especially with the new position but that wasn't what bothered her. What bothered her was his whole demeanor. Where he used to revel in her presence there were times now she wondered if he paid any more attention to her than the clock on the wall. And now this! Three o'clock in the morning with that bullshit about Samantha, an off-duty copy and a potential car-jacking. Who was he kidding? No there was something he was hiding and she was certainly going to find out what it was. After all Sylvia Stanton was nobody's fool.

Sitting on the edge of the bed Sylvia began mulling over the puzzle slowly and methodically seeing the best way to decipher the situation and putting all the pieces into play and all the potential threats into motion. Had there been any new players since her trip to North Carolina? She thought long and hard and the only one she could come up with was the new file clerk he'd mentioned once or twice in passing conversation. What was her name? Melissa, Michelle? No. Mindy. That was it. He'd spoken once or twice but always in a condescending tone. But then why would he speak of her in any other way especially if that's where his interests lay. Maybe to his office buddies and cohorts but he was too smart to speak of her in any way but with disdain when speaking to his wife. He was too smart to throw up an alert about some recent hire that he'd taken a fancy too. Still, he did admit that she was a beautiful girl and only a man with blinders on turned a deaf ear to beauty. And he after all a man and most men weren't guided by what was between the ears but what was between the legs. Still, she couldn't be sure.

And then there was Samantha or Sammy as he liked to call her but Sammy had long since been reduced to a non-threat. At first she had watched the progression of Samantha and the relationship between this bright and articulate White girl with the Tufts education and the beautiful body that made even Syl a little jealous but Samantha had always been straightforward, professional and respectful of both Syl and her marriage and if it weren't for Anthony's no fraternizing she gathered that they probably would have become close friends. They still talked without Anthony's knowledge but certainly not as much as she would have liked but if anyone would have noticed and questioned the sudden change in Anthony's demeanor it would be Samantha. A lunch date was long overdue and Syl smiled at the thought of seeing her old friend again.

Showering quickly, Syl's thoughts reverted back to Anthony. She had to admit that in their twelve year marriage he had never given her any reason to doubt him and had lived up to all of her expectations and doted on her. She was probably just feeling a tad bit insecure with the age difference and walking around with all this added weight. Then again her hormones could just be all out of whack and she was probably imagining things that really didn't exist but whatever it was for some reason it just didn't seem right and as she picked up the tiny cell phone she decided it was her duty and her right to reassure herself.

"Morning. Thanks for calling the offices of Mitchell & Ness. How may I help you this morning?"

Came the cheerful voice on the other end of the line.

"Morning sweetie. How are you this morning?"

The voice on the other end shook Samantha to her very core but professional as always she maintained her décor and answered as promptly as she could under the circumstances.

"What can I say? It's Friday and I'll be so glad when this week is over."

"I hear you girl."

"I take it you want to speak to Anthony. What did he forget today?"

"Actually I called to speak to you."

Samantha was on the edge of her seat now the bead of perspiration gathering together on the bridge of her nose.

"Well, that's good 'cause he's not in yet and he has an office full waiting to see him."

"He's not there yet? He should have been there. He left close to an hour ago."

"Don't worry about it Syl. Traffic may be bad around the tunnels and you know how Anthony is. He could be right down the block at that little bodega he loves so much a bagel in one hand and a regular coffee in the other hand talking about what the Knicks did last night."

"You're right. I guess it's just me. I'm running around here all out of sorts since I found out I was pregnant. All I do is worry. I don't know what's wrong with me."

Samantha was stunned. Pushing her chair back she dropped her head between her legs and gasped but no matter how hard she tried she could not for the life of her catch her breath.

"Samantha are you there? Samantha."

"Sorry Syl I got something caught in my throat. Go ahead what were you saying?"

"I said ever since I found out I was pregnant I've been moody and suspicious of everyone and everything. And so you know who comes at the top of the list."

"Well, congratulations Syl. I couldn't be happier for you," Samantha lied as the tears Kingd down her face.

"You mean Anthony didn't tell you?"

"Never mentioned a word."

"See that's what I'm talking about. For ten years the man asked me to grant him a son and after exercising and taking every type of fertility drug known to man and finally getting pregnant he acts likes he's changed his mind and could care less. He's just different. Call it a woman's intuition. Call it a hormonal change but something's gone left 'cause it just ain't right. Have you noticed any change in behavior on his part Sam?"

"No, not that I can put a finger on aside from the fact that he's a little quieter these days. He doesn't laugh and joke as much anymore. You know it's like he's lost some of his spontaneity."

"Do you think think it's the new position?"

"I'm pretty sure that has a lot to do with it. The added responsibility of the partnership along with maintaining his client base has to be overwhelming but he seems to be handling it well. Well, at least as well as can be expected for just having stepped into the position. But I will tell you this, most men would be here in the office 'til eleven or twelve each night with the workload Anthony has. I left here last night at around eight and he walked me to my car only to go back in the office. Said he had some work to do."

"He told me about your little ordeal last night."

"Oh my God. Not one of those things I want to recall. Can we talk about something else?"

"Sure darling I quite understand. So tell me about the new girl. I hear she's quite the looker."

"Oh, you must be talking about Mindy. She's gorgeous Syl. She makes us look like the two stepdaughters in Cinderella. I mean this girl has drop dead good looks. You know that all natural Cover girl look."

"She's Black?"

"Yes, and as sweet as she Anthony doesn't like her. And to be truthful with you I think he's the only person in the agency that has found fault with her. She's the cutest little thing. I think she said she's a senior at N.Y.U. I'm telling you Syl she's beautiful. I'll invite her the next time you and I have lunch."

"Sounds good to me. Actually that's what I was calling about but you've told me just about everything I wanted to know," she laughed. "I don't know what I would do without you Sam."

"Anytime. Gotta keep the old boy running right don't we?"

"I know that's right. Even the best men have a little wolf in them so ya gotta keep them on a tight leash," she remarked laughing again. "Well, I thank you for all of your insight Sam and keep me posted if there's anything you think I should know about?"

"I always do and congrats on your pregnancy Syl. I wish you the best. Oh, and since we're on the subject there is something I want you to look into."

"Yeah, what's that?"

"Well, there's a guy that Anthony's been meeting with over the past three or four months. His name is Joseph Assante but he is in no way connected to anything to do with Mitchell & Ness. An unsavory sort who dresses in five to six hundred dollar suits and well call it a woman's intuition but he just comes across as shady and when I asked Anthony the nature of their business he blew me off and Mr. Assante gave me one of those 'if I tell you I've got to kill you answers.'"

"Seriously?"

"Yes, and for some reason when he said it sent shivers through me. I mean that's the way he comes across. Just an unsavory type. Anyway when that whole horrible incident took place last night with those thugs in the parking garage don't you know he was there Johnny on the spot, sawed off shotgun in hand at the ready. I'm telling you Syl he's so unsettling that he scared the thieves."

Syl laughed.

"He's an off duty cop Samantha. Anthony told me all about how he rescued you two."

"Off duty cop my ass. Believe what you want I'm telling you he's a hood, a gangsta. That's what he is and he's not anybody Anthony should be involved with. Just take your time and be subtle and find out who he is. That's all I ask. Will you do that for me."

"He really has you shook doesn't he?"

"A bit."

"Okay, I'll see what I can find out."

"Thanks Syl."

"Not a problem. And you keep an eye on that Mindy heifer. I think there may be a little more going on than what Anthony is letting onto. By the way, what do you know about this Baltimore trip to see Boots?"

"Don't know too much about it other than he's flying down to finally close the account. Boots is a tough one for Ant. You know he's been working on it for more than a year."

"Yeah, I know well. I think he may get it this time though. I certainly hope so. I think it's a little more personal than business at this point. Sorta like his own little personal crusade. It's that male ego thing."

"I know."

"Are you going?" Samantha already knew the answer but had to make sure to cover all bases just in case.

"Please. Not to sit down with those stuffed shirts while they talk shop. No, my girlfriends and I are going up to Greenwich, Conneticut for their annual wine tasting fest. We go every year. You should come. We have a blast every time we go."

"Sorry but I promised mommy I would take her shopping this weekend."

"Oh yeah. Where are you going?"

"Cherry Hill Mall."

"Get out. Y'all ain't playing are you?"

Samantha laughed.

"Let me get off. Mr. Man just walked in the door and he ain't lookin' all too happy to be here."

"Mr. Man don't hardly look happy anymore. Tell him I said to get over it. I'll talk to you later Samantha."

"Be good," Sammy said staring at Anthony in his charcoal grey suit that hugged him just the way Sammy liked to.

Making his rounds and saying a little something or another he finally made his way around to Sammy who he winked at before picking up his daily itinerary.

"Mr. Roberts would you step into my inner sanctum," Anthony said opening the door for the elderly gentleman.

By twelve noon the office was empty and he turned to Samantha. The last order of business were the clients he intended on taking with him to Pendleton and Associates. There were forty who he was almost positive would follow and he double checked to see that meetings were set up for Monday, Tuesday and Wednesday of the following week. That secure he pulled the blinds on the Louvre doors and walked around the mahogany desk which Samantha adorned put his arms around her and squeezed her tightly.

"You ready to go lover?"

"To the depths of hell as long as it's with you, my sweetness."

"Then let's do the damn thing then, "Anthony said doing a two-step, swinging Sammy out and then pulling her back into the closeness of his arms.

"You do that well."

"And that's not all. Gotta few more steps I'd like to introduce you to."

"Oh, so we're going dancing,"

"In a manner of speaking."

"Well, baby you lead and I'll pick up some things along the way."

"I'm sure you will."

The flight was a small commercial one and before they could get seated comfortably they were instructed to put their seats in an upright position.

After claiming their bags they were both pleasantly surprised to find Boots limo waiting outside the airport terminal. He and the limo were on a first name basis and hugged like old friends.

"You gonna go far Mr. Pendleton. I tells Boots that all the time. That's what I like about you Mr. Pendleton. A lot of these here CEO's 'spects for you to hold the door which I don't mind doin' but they acts like you ain't no more'n gum on the bottom of they shoes. Half of 'em don't speak and don't wanna acknowledge nobody like me. Dey too high up and stuck on theyselves. What dey don't know is that Boots and I grew up together and he pays me more than they pay the senor brokers. But dey don't know dat. Shit! When I come outta high school I had a four year scholarship to go to Howard. Wanted to be a doctor but I ran into a little trouble and lost it."

"What happened?" Samantha asked.

"Me and Boots went to this little hole-n-da wall and Boots got into it wit' some of the local toughs. So, I went to his aid and broke a chair ova one of dem ofays heads."

"So what happened?" Samantha said goading the man on.

"What happened? Why I killed the boy and got sentenced to do an eight year bid. That's what happened. Now ya see if that same crime had happened right here in Baltimore it might have been considered self-defense but Boots was likin' this ofay over there in Prince George's County. I believe that's considered Virginia and back then you wasn't color mixin' and so I did some time. Came out with nothin'. No scholarship, couldn't get a job, nothin'. But Boots neva forgot me for savin' his life and done took care of me ever since."

"And?" Samantha said teasing.

"And I learned that if you is in your right mind you don't go chasin' no ofay womens." He said before bursting out laughing. The car filled with laughter as Ant and Sammy joined in.

"Touche," Sammy answered wiping the tears from her eyes.

"Although I might just change my mind if ever I met a White woman as purty as you but up to this point I ain't met one quite that purty," he said chuckling at his own joke.

"Thanks for the compliment and nice meeting you." Samantha said shaking the older man's hand.

"Duke's the name. And this is all mine," he said waving his hands all around. "I am the King of East Baltimore. Just ask your boy," he said winking at Samantha before turning and hugging Anthony.

"Call me Ant if you need one of the boys to come run ya 'round the city. All expenses paid. You know the Duke has ya while you're here. Don't let me here 'bout you paying fo' no cab."

"Thanks Duke."

The old man smiled before climbing into the Lincoln Navigator and swerving out into the busy Baltimore traffic.

"Come on sweetie. The hotel's right over here."

Samantha stood there and stared at Anthony.

"Anthony did you pay that old man?"

"Pay Duke," he asked incredulously.

"Well, did you even bother to tip him?"

"Tip him? Baby, were you listening. I believed he introduced himself as the King of East Baltimore. That man could buy and sell both you and I. If he spits here shit rattles and people start running for cover in east L.A. That's how much power that man wields. He alone could finance the firm I'm trying to open."

"That old man?"

"Yes, that old man."

The two entered the hotel and all eyes turned to the stately couple.

"Mr. Pendleton. Right on time as usual. How have you been sir? Oh, and congratulations on your promotion."

"I'm in 407 with the Jacuzzi?"

"Just as you ordered."

Anthony fished around in his wallet looking for the gold Visa card. Finding it he slid it to John who seeing it slid it right back.

"The Duke has paid your bill in advance sir."

"And how much is the suite we're staying in?"

"With all amenities included it runs around six seventy five a night."

"Higher than the Ritz Carlton?"

"The Ritz Carlton is a name. We are an experience. You will find that the Ritz Carlton can't touch us. But then why are you asking when you have stayed at both? I would be even so bold as to say that there is no finer hotel on the East Coast."

"Thanks John."

"Not a problem Mr. Pendleton. Should you need anything just call."

Grabbing Sammy's hand he led her through the lobby and towards the elevators.

"That was a lesson for you my dear."

"I got it."

"And that is..."

"To never judge a book by its cover..."

Anthony kissed Sammy and immediately felt himself drawn to her but there was no time.

"I want you Anthony."

"I want you too baby but I want you to see some things first. Have you ever been to Baltimore?"

"Passed by but can't say I've ever actually had a chance to see the city?"

"Well, Miss Thang you are in for the time of your life."

"Sounds like a plan," Samantha said as they entered the room. "But first I think we need to talk."

"About?"

"A few things lover. Syl called me this morning. That's who I was on the phone with when you walked in. She was quite inquisitive."

"Oh yeah," Anthony said matter-of-factly as he opened several tiny bottles at the mini bar. "I'm not sure how this works anymore Sammy. Would a glass of wine be better for you?"

"Wine is fine. Anyway she said you've not been the same since your trip to North Carolina or since our first encounter and is hot on the pursuit of another woman although at this time she's barking up the wrong tree. She really thinks its Mindy."

"Who? Not the little half-wit file clerk that just started," Anthony said angrily. "Why would she stick me with her of all people?"

"Be nice Ant and just be grateful for small blessings. She could have thought it was me."

"You're right."

"Well, anyway she asked me to keep an eye out on you."

"That's like telling the fox to watch the hen house," Anthony laughed as he sipped his drink, handed Sammy a glass of wine and called downstairs to the front desk.

"Hello John. Can u send someone up to grab some clothes I need them clean and pressed by eight tonight. Okay. Thank you. You were saying..."

"Nothing. That was all," Samantha replied as she gazed into the glass of wine. "Anthony why didn't you tell me Syl was pregnant?"

"Not something I like to think about," he said nonchalantly.

"So what are you planning on doing?"

"What can I do? My hands are basically tied. She thinks she's giving me something I desire and I do want a child. I just don't want her to be the mother of my child."

"Well, I seriously doubt that she wants another little one. I know she loves her son but she doesn't want the responsibility of taking care of him and the only reason she's having this one is because she thinks you want it."

"And when we divorce I will take him as well. Did she also tell you that she raised a little over two million to get the firm up and running?"

"No she didn't. Did she really?"

"In a week. The woman actually scares me. She simply has too much power and you know what they say about a woman's wrath. Lord knows what she would do if she were to find out about us."

Sammy smiled.

"You're making my nature rise. Just the thought of doing something obscene and wrong makes my kitty purr," Sammy laughed.

""You have issues, Sammy."

"Nothing the good doctor can't fix."

"You right. You wanna grab a bite to eat?"

"Thought you were having dinner with Boots?"

"Thatt's tomorrow. Tonight I'm having lunch and a late night dinner with the prettiest young lady in all of Baltimore."

"Oh, that is so sweet."

"You feel like walking."

"You lead. I will follow."

The couple left the hotel hand in hand and across the street to the inner harbor and down the steps to Phillip's Crab Shack where they ate crab legs and drank Coronas until the early evening when Anthony took her hand and walked the length of the inner harbor at times stopping, and turning to face each other and kissing each other lightly, tenderly. At around seven the couple crossed over to the other side of the inner harbor and entered Barnes & Noble bookstore. Both had a fascination for books and once inside they parted ways agreeing to meet at a small table on the second floor. An hour later the table was stacked with books and anyone looking on would never have known the two were together as each was in their own world content. It was not until the announcement was made that either looked up and by then the sun had settled and the inner had grown quiet except for the young lovers who adorned it kissing and hugging as young lovers do.

"How are you feeling Sammy?"

"I've never felt better," Sammy said holding his hand in both of hers and looking up at him as if the entire world revolved around him.

"You want to do anything special love?"

"Go back to the room with the man I love would be my wish if I had my way."

"Then to the room it is he said," pulling Dukes card and his cell from his pocket.

"No, baby it's a beautiful night let's walk."

Arriving at the hotel twenty minutes later the couple entered the hotel lobby to the sweet sounds of a jazz trio playing Wynton Kelly. Samantha was immediately drawn in and pulled Anthony to a seat at the far end of the lobby.

"Can we listen for a few minutes?"

Anthony, almost as mesmerized as she was by the melodic chords made himself comfortable ordering a Chivas Regal on the rocks. Two hours later the band started packing up and the two made their way to the elevator and their room. Kissing him lightly on the neck as he slid the key in the door it was obvious what her intent was and by the time he had the door open and he was inside he was almost fully disrobed and she was on him.

"My God! You don't know how bad I've wanted you. I was dreaming of this the whole time I was down at the harbor. Those kisses on the pier set me off but I didn't want to seem too forward or I would have seduced you right there," she said smiling playfully.

"Wish you had. Funny, I had those same thoughts."

"Think we'll always feel this way about each other."

"I can't call it Sammy but I know how I feel right now so let's not waste words or time."

The two struggled to undress each other and the conversation between the two could have made for no better foreplay as Anthony forced his way into her warm, wet vagina.

Five minutes later they lay there panting and spent when a knock came from the door.

"Think we made too much noise."

"Don't think it was me per se," Anthony said laughing as he grabbed the terry cloth robe. "I thought you made enough noise to raise the dead."

Samantha to see who it was grabbed a towel and wrapped it around her so she could peek around the bedroom door and see if someone had indeed complained. She had never been a screamer—well not in her one other sexual encounter—but Anthony brought the best out of her and much as she did to hold her own he took her to places she'd never known and well it just came out.

Anthony cracked the door.

"It's done," was all she managed to hear but that voice, she recognized that voice. She couldn't place it but she definitely recognized.

"Who was that?"

"That was the Duke."

"Well, what did he want?"

"Just being the Duke I guess. Asked if we wanted a tour of East Baltimore."

"Should I get dressed?"

"No sweetie, I told him we'd take a rain check and go tomorrow night. But if you're up to it we can go tonight."

"No. That's fine. You wore my ass out."

"I sure hope not. We only played the first half. We still have the second half to look forward to," Anthony laughed.

"You're crazy as hell."

"I'm dead serious."

"Oh, so you brought me to Baltimore to screw my brains out is that it. I'm starting to wonder about you. I'm beginning to believe that all you want me for is to dip your wick and answer the phone for you. Is that it?"

"Damn, I was wondering how long I could hold you off and keep you at bay. But you figured it out didn't you"

"Go to hell Ant."

Anthony laughed.

"Seriously though, what are your intentions concerning me and the baby? You know through all of our time together you have yet to bring up either me or the baby and what part we play in your busy life. But you know I have a life too and God knows I never thought I'd be saying this but a lot of what I do and what direction my life now takes is contingent on you."

"Sammy, don't get the wrong impression and understand this if you don't understand anything else. I love you and if you'll just bear with me I think all of your questions will be answered tomorrow after I meet with Boots."

"Okay, I'm lost. Are you saying your meeting with Boots is the deciding factor on whether I'll have you for a lifetime or not. I don't get it. I don't understand."

"I know you don't baby and no Boots doesn't have a dam thing to do with any of this but after dinner with Boots tomorrow evening I think I can answer any questions you may have concerning you and the baby."

"Is that right?"

"My word to you love. Just hold on a little longer."

Chapter 8

The following day, a brisk one started just as the
evening before ended with Samantha wanting nothing
more than her man to love her. Anthony, always one
to placate spent most of the morning trying to appease
the demons that had been consuming her since she'd
fallen in love with Anthony seven years ago. When it
was over and Samantha was asleep Anthony showered
and dressing as not to disturb her wrote her a short
note before heading down to the hotel lobby. Now a

little after noon he made his way to the bar in lounge and ordered a double Jack and made a phone call.

Moments later a long black limo pulled up outside of the hotel. Sliding in he greeted Boots but it was all business now and there were no smiles.

"How did it go down?"

"Smooth as silk. Joe's a professional. You give him your mark and just let him do what he does best. Called me last night. He's funny though. Boy has a thing about phones. Made me go buy one of those throw away phones and then called me back to say he posed as a limo driver, picked the old man up at the airport and stopped on the way. Told the old man he had to piss then walked around the back of the car and gave him two to the back of the head. Left him out there in the swamps by Kennedy. Nothing to it. It's done. How are you and the little lady doing?"

"She's good. Sleeping soundly."

"You rocked her to sleep?"

"Something like that."

"She's a pretty girl."

"That she is."

"And married to a very rich man."

"Hopefully, although I'm not sure about the marriage part just yet."

"I hear you. You know thirty years ago when I was about your age I wouldn't have even entertained dating a White girl. I didn't have the heart. Valued my life too much. And I never did. My boy Boots did and I did the time for him but you know I don't know if it's the wisdom of old age or pure unadulterated stupidity but if were you and I loved a woman as I think you love this one I'd be damned if I let society dictate who and what I love? If they ain't ready that's their fault. Let 'em catch up."

"I hear you but in lieu of the firm and the investors being all-White if I do decide to make that move I want to make sure I have their confidence."

"And their dollars."

"That too."

Both men laughed.

"Listen, young buck. You know both me and Boots got your back. I want the first option to buy in though after this here thing blows over. You know the bottom's gonna fall out of Mitchell & Ness' stocks for a while, and you may even lose a few of your investors after they learn of his untimely death but once you stabilize things and they see that his death was nothing more than a bump in the road and they find out that one of the hottest young prospects on Wall Street has taken the reigns they're going to go through the roof."

"Let's hope so.
        "Trust the wisdom of an old man," Duke laughed. "Say you ever read Macchiavelli's The Prince boy?"

"Glanced through it once or twice."

"Should read. It's all about power. Hate to say it but it's my bible. Just helps me to understand the world better. Let me just give you one example of how it works. A government is in place and it's working fine. It's taking care of itself. Those in charge are getting wealthy beyond your wildest imagination and the guy next door is profiting too. Now one day the leader of that nation says he wants to control everything including the monies and decides to cut everyone off that he's been sharing with. Well, what do you think happens then?"

"I suppose they vote him out of office."

Duke laughed a deep resounding heartfelt laugh.

"Boy you may have the no how to run a firm but you a little light in the pants when it comes to knowing how the powers that be run things," he said choking on his own words. "No, my brother. When the power gets to the point when he wants to stop paying tithes they get rid of him and put in a government that will serve their pockets. That's exactly what happened to Saddam Hussein. You know he was an ally of the United States for the longest time but when he bucked the system and started questioning his paying tithes you see what they did to him. They took him out. And that's why Boots decided it was the right time for Mr. Mitchell to give up the throne. He'll make the deal now that you're in there but he wasn't ever going to make the deal with Mitchell or Ness. You feel me?"

"I feel you."

"And Ant if there's one thing I want you to understand and believe."

"What's that Duke?"

"I wanted you to know what was going to happen before it did so it didn't take you under like that undertow out there in Baltimore Harbor but don't you even think that because you knew that you had anything to do with it. You didn't. That was all Boots. He's been thinking about this shit for year but when Ness died and you stepped up to the plate he just saw it as an opportune time to step to the plate. But don't you think that you were in anyway were responsible for Mitchell's demise. A murder is a terrible thing to carry around with you for the rest of life. Ask me I know. You understand me Anthony?"

"I do."

"Marry that fine ass White girl. Work hard for about another five years and find you a nice little cottage down in the Bahamas and spend the rest of your life sippin' Pina Coladas on the beach and lovin' that woman."

"I hear you."

"Listen I set up everything at Attman's and I'll be around at somewhere around seven thirty to pick you up."

"Thanks Duke."

"Never a problem. And listen I hope you don't mind but I took the liberty of telling Boots your plans and he said all you have to do is send the papers and he'll sign so if you want to give them to me and I'll get his signature and return them to you this evening when I pick you up."

"Sounds like a plan to me."

"All I want from you is to let me know when you expect those stocks to soar. You know when they recover from the nosedive they're about to take. I believe they call that insider trading," he said laughing.

"How could I forget?"

"See you at seven thirty."

Anthony returned to the hotel but did not go directly to the bar. There were so many things going on in his mind that he didn't know where to start when it came to sorting them out. He didn't know if he should share with Samantha what he knew of Mr. Mitchell's murder but thought it best to roll with the flow. He had received no phone call so in essence how would he know of it. He was sure if no one called him before the night was over he would read it in tomorrow's paper just like everyone else. He had an airtight alibi but now wondered if it were smart to be in a hotel with his secretary should the police come to question him as they certainly would. Still, if he were to change rooms it would certainly arouse suspicion in Sammy's eyes and in itself be an admission of guilt. Then there was the matter of Samantha who now openly admitted she loved him and was pregnant with his child. Was she looking for marriage? He who once believed that marriage was all that he needed to complete him now wondered about the whole idea of the institution of marriage. And should he choose to marry again it certainly wouldn't be right after leaving his first wife. That was for damn sure. Why compound one mistake on top of another. What he needed was time to sort the whole thing out but no one seemed to be able to afford him the time he so sorely needed. And then there was Syl who presented the most difficult challenge of all. Divorce was imminent but the fact that she was pregnant and had ultimately done so because he'd at one time thought the idea of having a child was a good idea only added to the dilemma that faced him. And then there was all the pain and trauma that Syl had experienced at the hands of men. It had taken him considerable time and countless therapy sessions prior to their marriage and who knew how many promises that he was different and would never hurt her. And now here she was four months pregnant and know it or not on the verge of divorce. There was one positive where Syl was concerned though. With Mitchell's murder he no longer needed the two million she had in her possession as startup money. There was no need to open a firm of his own now. Mitchell and

Ness despite the name was essentially his. The board members would certainly ratify him as CEO. In the four months since he'd become partner they'd seen their revenues increase by close to twenty five percent which meant millions of dollars in their pockets no they would certainly ratify him as long as he continued to line their pockets. A Herculean task in front of him Anthony downed the last of the Patron in front and stood up on wobbly legs and headed for the elevators but not before he was approached by two men leaving the front desk.

"Anthony Pendleton?"

"Yes sir. Who may I ask is inquiring?"

"Detective Lasko and Detective Mirelli. May we have a few words with you Mr. Pendleton?"

"Certainly detectives. What's this all about?"

Anthony remained standing.

"You may want to have a seat."

"I'm fine sir."

"Have it your way," the stockier of the two detectives said. "It seems that your boss Mr. Mitchell has been murdered."

"What!?!?" Anthony said the shock and disbelief evident. Falling backwards as much from the Patron and Jack Daniels as from the news both detectives grabbed Anthony to break his fall and eased him onto one of the lobbies many couches.

"What happened? No, you must be mistaken. I just met with him yesterday morning in my office. He was leaving for Boston and was just making sure that everything was in order."

"All that checks out and although we have to follow through on all leads we are not looking at you as a suspect but we do need to ask you some questions with the hopes that you can shed some light on this most grievous crime."

"I'll tell you all if it'll help you apprehend the person that did this."

The grilling went on for close to half an hour and ended with both detectives satisfied.

"This is a pretty high profile case so we may around again as we gain leads."

"Not a problem. I'm glad I could be of some help detectives."

The whole affair was startling. Sure he had known but when Duke told him it was almost like part of normal conversation no more or less important than how many Melo had against the Celtics. The detectives however brought it all home. And he had to admit that he was now shaken.

"Hey honey. Where did you go?"

"Just met with an old friend. You were sleeping so I didn't want to bother you."

"Female?"

"What are you asking me?"

"You know what I'm asking you. Was you're old friend of the female persuasion?"

"No, it was just Duke. Went down and had a couple of drinks with him is all."

"A couple of drinks? You look like you had more than just a couple. More like a couple of bottles. Are you okay?"

"Yeah! Well, no. On the way back in I was stopped by a couple of detectives. They had some rather disturbing news."

By the time Anthony finished recounting what the detectives had told him Samantha sat there speechless.

"I'll be back," he muttered quietly.

"Where are you going baby?"

"Just gonna take a quick shower and get some of these cobwebs out of my head."

"Are you alright, baby?"

"Yeah, I'm fine."

"Leave the water running baby."

No sooner had Anthony grabbed a towel than the tiny cell started to chirp.

"Hello."

"Hey baby. How are you? I thought you were going to call me as soon as you down to let me know you arrived safely. You see that's why I can't let you out of my sight. What is they say? Out of sight out of mind. Hold on your son wants to say hello." There was a long pause before Syl returned. "Did you talk to him? You know I was reading this New Parent magazine and they say that as early as three months a child will respond to the sound of its parent's voice. Anthony are you there?"

"I'm here."

"You're awfully quiet. I guess you got the news."

"Yeah, I got it. Two detectives just stop by to question me."

"Are you okay?"

"I'm still in a state of shock but you know me. I'll survive."

"I think you're looking at this the wrong way love. There's two ways to look at it. You can look at it as the glass being half empty or half full. If you look it as being half empty then yes you'll survive but if you look at it as being half full then you have to smile at the thought of you having sole command of your ship."

"Only you would think of ways you can benefit from a man's murder. If I didn't know about your distaste for blood and guns I'd consider you the prime suspect in his murder," Anthony decreed.

Syl laughed.

"I wouldn't say I'm pleased to hear to hear about his death but I think a little faster than your normal person and while you're still deliberating his death I've already finished the grieving process and moved on. My next question is what it means for those that still are alive and my husband in particular."

"I feel you. Did you call Mrs. Mitchell and wish her your condolences?"

"You already know that. Sent her flowers too."

"Okay, I need to do the same. See you tomorrow night love."

"I love you Anthony."

"Love you too baby."

Anthony proceeded to call Mrs. Mitchell and offer her condolences before jumping in the shower. The warm was soothing and relaxing and he stayed in so long that Sammy came to check and see if he was alright.

"The water feels good baby," was all he could manage to say. It was true that the day had already taken its toll on him. Samantha recognizing so let her gown fall to the floor before stepping in.

"What can I do to please you baby," she said kneeling before him.

"Nothing baby. I just need a nap and I'll be as good as new. Between you and the news of Mr. Mitchell I'm beat." He said stepping out and handing her the soap.

"Wow! This is the first time you've ever turned me down. Doesn't make a girl feel very loved."

"Not turned down just postponed," Anthony said grabbing her by the shoulders and kissing her passionately. "Listen my credit card is on the dresser by my wallet. If you're in the mood you can walk down to the harbor. There's a mall directly across the street. They tell me it's an upscale woman's fantasy. Why don't you treat yourself? Tell me there's a Coach store and a perfume palace. Go and enjoy yourself. Splurge! And do me a favor find a cute little outfit for dinner tonight. Nothing fancy but chic and elegant. Will you do that for me?"

"Anything for my knight in shining armor."

Five minutes later Anthony was sound asleep.

He awoke and found that dusk had fallen as he gazed out the window. And although he could make out the smooth sounds of Coltrane's Ballads playing in the next room it was quiet. Pulling himself from the bed he had to admit the nap had done him a world of good. He was somehow refreshed. Splashing the cold water on his face brought him back and he thought of the news he'd received earlier and was strangely taken back by the melancholy mood that came over him. He'd never been able to deal with death even from afar but when it was this close and touched him it was something altogether different. In a very real sense Mr. Mitchell had been a mentor, a sort of father figure to him teaching him the ins and outs and the shortcuts. If nothing else he respected him and attributed much of his success to him. And now he was gone.

Anthony took the Chivas from the bar, grabbed a glass and headed for the loveseat where he poured a healthy shot and sipped slowly.

Sammy was still gone and for the first time he was glad. He needed some quiet time some peace from other's needs. Putting his head back he let the Chivas course through his body and enjoyed the warm sensation.

His peace was short lived as moments later Sammy came bounding through the door bags in both hands followed by the bell hop and the consigliore all with as many bags as she and smiles almost as wide as hers. Her infectious personality and down-to-earth personality seemed to have the same effect on everyone that came into contact with her and it was just one of the many things Anthony loved about her.

"Baby I went in there with the idea of just picking up an outfit and lost my mind. My God! And they say New York and Paris are the fashion capitols. Well, Baltimore ain't far behind! And the prices... Oh my God!! I had to keep looking over my shoulder for the security guard. Felt like I was stealing. And you should see what I got!" Sammy said as she pulled two fives out of her wallet tipping the two men who still stood there smiling at the bubbly young lady standing before them.

"Thank youma'm," they both said. "Enjoy your stay and if there's anything else you may need just give me a call," the older gentleman said giving his card to Anthony.

Sammy ignored the man so intent was she on showing Anthony the buys she'd gotten.

"Stop! Stop!" Anthony said smiling and closing the door behind the two men.

Sammy stood there like a small child denied her popsicle before dinner.

"But..."

"No buts...Fix yourself a drink and hurry and get changed. We're running late. Duke'll be here in less than five minutes and the man is prompt and doesn't like to be kept waiting."

Sammy poured some more in Anthony's now empty glass and threw it back before pouring herself another which she sipped more slowly.

"I thought I asked you to go out and grab an outfit for tonight?"

"I did." Sammy said a little taken back by Anthony's gruff tone.

"It doesn't take six and a half hours to find an outfit. And not only didn't you just go out and grab an outfit it looks more like you tried to purchase the whole goddamn store."

"What is this about?" Sammy said growing angry now. "I believe you were the one who told me to take your card and go out and splurge."

"Within reason is what I said since you want to quote me. Now would you please hurry? I told you the man's waiting. He's probably downstairs as we speak." And then as if that weren't enough he added a "Damn!" as Sammy turned and went into the bedroom to change.

Changing quickly Sammy didn't know what Anthony had in mind but one thing she did know was that whatever bug had crawled up his ass she wouldn't be treated like shit by him or any other man.

Putting on her black pumps to match her plain black dress she looked stunning.

"Let me tell you one thing Anthony Pendleton. I came because you invited me and I came to enjoy myself. I didn't come as your assistant and even if I did you and no other man is going to talk to me or disrespect me as you just did. If you look on the nightstand next to the bed you'll see that I never even touched your card. I spent my own damn money so I don't know why you're getting so upset."

"Why didn't you take my card like I asked you to?"

"How smart is that genius? All Syl has to do is check your credit card statement and see Coach and Tiffany's and that's your ass. Come on. Act like you know. And you sitting here trying to have a fuckin' attitude over something," she said spinning quickly and heading to the bar.

Ant dropped his head and smiled. Lord knows she was feisty.

"Just bring your ass on. Didn't I tell you the man is waiting," he said turning his head and walking to the door. He was still smiling, teasing her but she didn't know it.

"I don't know who you're talking to or what bug crawled up your ass but you can go the hell on. I'm really not feeling you tonight."

"Oh come on and stop acting like a spoiled little rich girl and bring your ass on."

Sammy was not to be treated just any kind of way and she made it a point to let Anthony know in the elevator and all the way to the car where Duke waited patiently.

"How you all good peoples doin' this evening," Duke said grinning. "You lookin' mighty fine there Ms. Samantha. If I was twenty years younger you'd have a fight on your hands boy."

"Thought you didn't date White women?" Samantha chimed in.

"B'lieve I'd have to make an exception in yo' case good as you look."

"Well thank you Sir Duke," Samantha cooed.

Ant beamed with pride knowing that the old man was on point. Another more insecure man may have taken offense with Duke's compliment but both men were assure of their own manhood and knew that the compliment was a testament not only to the woman standing in their midst but to the man who'd pulled her.

"Where we headed?" Duke said knowing full well where they were going.

"Altman's." Anthony replied.

"One of Baltimore's hidden treasures," the Duke said matter-of-factly. "Juniors is good but I'd put my money on Altman's all day and all night."

"I'd have to agree with you there," Ant replied.

"And after tonight I believe Ms. Sam may think it's the finest restaurant in the nation," he laughed.

"Okay what are you two up to?" Sammy said still not over her little ordeal with Anthony. Pulling up in front of the tiny delicatessen Samantha hardly knew what all the hoopla was about and as soon as she was inside she seriously wondered if the man she had been so taken with was working with a full deck. Sure the place was nice but a far cry from elegant and certainly not the type of place that called for her to put her pretty on. The smell of fish and dill pickles was overwhelming and the small deli was overcrowded with blue collar workers, some in carpenter's paints, and others in coveralls with paint splattered. Sammy didn't mind, after all she'd grown up in the lower middle class Ironbound section of Newark but what she did mind was Ant having her dress like she were going to some exclusive restaurant when in reality it was just a local deli. Food may have been to die for but it was still a deli. Anthony pulled her through the crowd until he found a table for two in the corner in the back and even this bothered Sammy. Why had he passed all those empty tables to drag her back here? He was suddenly acting like someone she hardly knew and wondered if he was ashamed to be seen with her but looking around she hardly saw what he could be ashamed of. And the crowd of people milling around or standing in line hardly took notice of them so busy were they to get their orders and get home from work.

"I'm going to have a pastrami and Swiss with mustard and a dill pickle with some chips and a large root beer. They have the best pastrami if I do say so myself. What can I get for you Sam?"

Sammy stared at him almost in disbelief before answering. Still at a loss as to what was truly happening she played along if only not to cause a scene. They'd already had words once today and she had no intentions of letting Anthony's antics ruin her weekend. The old man's death only meant more stress and responsibility and despite his cool demeanor she knew he was feeling the strain. And to top it off he had to deal with the fact that he had two powerful women pregnant and jockeying for position There was little doubt that all of this had to be an awful burden for one man to bear. Taking all this into consideration Sammy simply said.

"I'll have the same."

Anthony parted the loud raucous crowd and made his way to the men's room stopping the waitress on the way. Pointing at Sammy he placed the order and continued on. On his return, there was little in the way of conversation and Anthony remained resolute in his strange behavior. Despite Samantha's decision not to pry or to add to his worry she felt compelled to question about his behavior.

"Baby, are you alright?"

"I'm fine. Why do you ask?"

"Dunno. You just seem out of sorts today? Like something's really troubling you. I know Mr. Mitchell's death must be taking its toll on you but..."

"Ya think?"

"See what I'm saying Ant? You're so curt. I'm almost afraid to say anything to you for fear of an argument. You've got me walking on eggshells ever since I got back from the Inner Harbor."

Anthony smiled and took her free hand in his.

"I'm sorry baby. I'm just having a hard putting everything in perspective and believe it or not Mr. Mitchell's murder is not the most pressing thing on my mind today."

"Well, I thought you said Duke said that the Boots account was a given so I can't understand what else could possibly be bothering you. Have you talked to Syl today?"

"I did but she's the least of my worries. There are choices and decisions that a man makes that are often times life altering decisions and one that I made today falls in that category and so I guess I am a little out of sorts."

"Wanna share?"

"I will when the time is right."

"Didn't know we had any secrets," Samantha stated dejectedly.

"We don't. All things in time..."

As if on cue the redheaded waitress showed up with two plates overflowing with food.

"Thank you," Anthony said winking at the pretty young lady as he his food.

"I saw that mister," Sammy said smiling at Anthony. "A bit young for your tastes isn't she? I thought you were more inclined to the middle aged," she said grinning sheepishly.

"No, you didn't."

Sammy grinned. Her reference to Syl obvious.

"Think all that's about to change," he grinned back. "Come on Sammy eat. We've got too much on the agenda for me to be sitting here listening to your slick mouth.

"Is that right? I was kinda hoping you had something else in mind besides this little cheap ass deli you brought me to," she said grinning again.

"Oh no you didn't."

"Oh but I did and since we're on the subject why would you even tell me to go shopping and find an outfit to wear here. If I wanted to be stirred up and smell like fish I would have preferred it to be my own," she replied still grinning and forgetting everything that was bothering her in lieu of the man that sat across from her.

"Would you stop with the wise cracks and eat please."

Sammy stared at the food in front of her.

"What? My hips aren't big enough and my ass ain't round enough? Tryin' to turn your White girl into a sister? Is that it?" Sammy said staring at Anthony who broke out laughing.

"What the hell hasn't gotten in to you? What did you have today? Now I'm thinking I should have gone with you when you went shopping or I should have had Duke escort you."

"Please. I wish I did have something. Wish I had a man that gave it to me on the regular then maybe I wouldn't be so damn hyped."

"Hold up missy? What is it that you're inferring? Are you saying that I don't meet your needs?"

Samantha smiled.

"Did I strike a nerve?"

"No, just trying to get you to expound."

"Just saying that most men wouldn't deny me when I come into the shower naked and ask my man to take care of my needs."

"Oh, this is about this afternoon?"

"No, this is about a man who ain't taking care of his business."

Anthony was smiling.

"Perhaps if my lady friend would bring something new to the table then I might be interested in tapping that ass a little more frequently."

"If you had more than that three inches you're packin' you might find some new stuff here," she said staring at him without even a trace of a smile.

Anthony damn near fell off of his chair in laughter.

"Never had any complaints before. Just check the resume."

"I believe you. No need for me to do any research on that account. From what I can see with your interest in fourteen year old virgins like our waitress and senior citizens like Syl I can understand how they would be content with any type of penetration but we full fleged women need a bit more I'm afraid," she said now smiling.

"I'm so sorry Sammy that I don't have the motion for that ocean. You know and since we're being brutally honest I sometimes feel like those men who attempt to swim the English Channel. Sometimes I get out there and wonder if I'm going to drown because it's so damn wide and deep. And damn if I don't forget my lifejacket every time I get in the bed with you. You know my dad used to say I didn't have good sense and every time I get in the bed with you I realize he was telling the truth. A lot of the times when it's over I look up at the ceiling and ask myself, 'what the hell just happened'. I mean I know that you are new to sex and making love but they do have books on the subject you know," Anthony said laughing.

"Is that right?" she said sarcastically.

"Yeah and sex therapists who may be better able to tell you how to make that thing a tad bit more responsive 'cause I swear to you—since we're being honest and sharing—that I would seriously appreciate it if you could somehow wake that shit up. Is it comatose or what?"

"Five more inches of dick and it may just wake up. But most of the time you're rolling over and getting ready to light a cigarette and I'm wondering when you're going to put it in," Sammy laughed.

"C'mon now sweetie. Do you think I do for other women what I've done for you. I have never engaged in oral sex with all the women I've known as much as I have with you. And do you know why?"

"No, please tell me you sex god you."

"I have because I love you and—well it's sort of like performing last rights—you know mouth-to-mouth resuscitation is all the first aid I know. It's basically a last resort and the only way I know to try and bring that shit back to life."

Samantha threw the piece of pickle in her hand across the table hitting Anthony just above the eye. They both laughed.

"You know I never wanted to say anything but there were a few times I thought about call EMS 'cause I was sure it was dead but I never said anything. I just prayed."

They both were in tears now and neither could imagine being in anyone else's company.

"I love you Sammy."

"Not nearly as much as I love you. You can't even imagine how much I do."

"Take me back to the hotel and show me."

"Can't wait but first tell me how you liked the food?"

"I think I'm in agreement with Duke. Haven't had better. I wonder if I can have one of those pastrami and Swiss frozen and shipped back to mommy next day air."

"I suppose you could but if you think that was good then you have to try their chocolate cake. You know how Juniors claim to fame is their cheesecake well Altman's is known for their chocolate cake. It's ridiculous."

"Baby, did you see all the food on my plate. There's no way in hell."

"Listen. You just try it. Just take a bite and what you don't eat I will," Anthony said summoning the waitress over once more and ordering.

"What, no wink this time?"

"No, she got the message the first time. Don't want to overdo it. Gotta be easy. She knows the deal."

"You sure? I see you getting up at three in the morning I'll know the deal too. You'll be going back to New York three inches shorter."

Anthony laughed

"And you know what bothers me about that is that I kinda believe you."

"You should. I've always been the jealous type and I will lose it if I even think someone's getting too close to what's mine. I know there ain't no rhyme or reason but someone will get seriously hurt if they get in my space."

"I believe you too. No worries I only have eyes for you and I think Kathy will tell you that," Anthony said staring at the little red-haired waitress now who handed Samantha the silver tray. Samantha took the tray but her eyes never left Anthony who was still concentrating on the waitress.

"Is everything in order?"

"Just as you asked Mr. Pendleton."

Anthony could see the anger growing in Sammy and once again reached out and took her hand in his.

Smiling he pointed to the platter.

Sammy still taken by the little episode between Anthony and the waitress stared at Anthony.

"What the hell was that all about?"

"Taste the cake baby so we can get out of here."

"I'm not thinking about any damn cake or anything else right now. I want to know what's up with you and Barbie."

"If you take a bite of cake I'll answer all your questions."

"You and your damn cake," Samantha said lifting the top from the platter. In the center of the platter was a white doily and the largest diamond Samantha had ever seen. Samantha estimated it to be no less than four carats and was speechless."

"I hope this answers any questions you may have about you and I and the baby. To make a long story short, I love you Samantha and would be honored if you'd take my hand in marriage."

The tears Kingd down her face as she stared at Anthony.

"I don't know what to say," she stammered.

"Say yes," Anthony said beaming with pride.

"I am so happy for you," Kathy said embracing Samantha.

"Thank you so much."

"You still haven't answered." Anthony stated.

"I think the tears say it all," Kathy chimed in grinning like it was she who had been proposed to.

Duke waited outside and joined in the festivities.

"I guess I was the only one who didn't know," Samantha said as Duke hugged and congratulated her. "Where to?"

"Anywhere the lady wants to go," Anthony stated matter-of-factly.

"I'd like to go back to the room."

"You don't want to go out and celebrate?"

"No, I've had enough excitement for one day. All I want to do is lay it down and try to fathom what just happened," she said grinning as the tears Kingd down her face once more.

Anthony lost track of how many times they made love that night and each time he rolled over and tried to sleep she was crying and tearing at him wanting more. And it was like from Saturday evening until Sunday when Duke drove them to the airport.

Chapter 9

Mondays were always hectic and this one was even
more chaotic than most with the news of Mr.
Mitchell's untimely demise. Anthony almost hated the
thought of going into the office. After the weekend
he'd just had he knew he could have been a shoe in as
a finalist on Survival if he could manage to just get
through this one.

A light drizzle fell and only dampened his spirits even more as he pulled into the parking garage a block away from the office. Sliding out he felt sore. Women were funny and it was almost as if Syl could sense something this morning as she mounted him and rode him as if there were no tomorrow. She said it was her gift to the new senior partner of Mitchell & Ness but all he could sense was that she was leaving her scent and marking her territory. And as much as he wanted to block it out all he could hear was her voice saying 'fuck me daddy'.

He did his best to shut out the voices in his head. And he wished hers was the only one he heard but he couldn't. There was Duke recounting the details of the murder and the two detectives in the Baltimore hotel lobby who assured him he was exonerated for now but would surely face more questions when he returned to New York. And of course there was Samantha who hadn't up 'til now questioned his timeline but who certainly would now that he'd proposed. It was all a bit much and then there was just the normal frantic and crazy pace that a normal day would bring.

If he'd been smart he'd have stopped off at his usual haunt and picked up a cup of coffee and gotten the skinny before he'd even thought about going in but it was a little too late for that now. Anthony felt the butterflies and suddenly felt more than a little nauseous on his way into the office. Stepping into the office he knew his fears were founded as the small lobby teemed with throngs of well-wishers and inquisitive clients curious to know where they stood and how their accounts would be affected now with Mr. Mitchell's death. Samantha was manning the phones which rang incessantly and seemed to be as stressed as he was.

"Morning Mr. Pendleton," she managed to get out before the phone rang again.

Anthony nodded before being bombarded by three or four nervous clients.

"Gentlemen, gentlemen," he said ignoring the anxious few and addressing the whole floor instead.

"I know you're all in a quandary as to what we're doing and in which direction Mitchell & Ness is moving following the sudden death of Mr. Mitchell and I have to admit that I am in a bit of a quandary myself but I have a board meeting at ten and I am really not at liberty to speak until I have met with the board. But if I were to venture to guess I would say that up 'til now you have all felt pretty good in your relationship with Mitchell & Ness and I see no reason why Mister Mitchell's untimely demise would affect business at the firm is done. If I were to prognosticate I would venture to say that things will stay the same. My father used to always say 'if it ain't broke don't ix it' and I see no reason to tamper with perfection. Now, if any of you have questions aside from the direction of Mitchell & Ness feel free to make yourselves comfortable and I will update you following the board meeting. I will, however fax each and every one of you the minutes of the meeting as soon as it's over if you have more pressing matters to deal with. Now if you'll excuse me I have a board meeting to attend. With that said Anthony exited the lobby. Stepping into the long hallway Anthony breathed a deep sigh of relief.

A moment later Samantha stood at his side.

"Had to come out here and check to see if I'd wet myself. Damn! You are one commanding presence. I started to ask for your autograph but I didn't want to interrupt. Ever thought of entering politics love?"

Anthony smiled glad that that was over but the board would be no easier and would be questioning his intentions and the direction he intended on taking the firm just as the clients had with the only difference being that they had the power to replace him if he wasn't in unison with the populous.

"Hey, Sammy this promises to be the week from hell and you can expect a lot of off the wall shit coming from who knows where but just keep your feet on the ground and your eyes on the prize. You know a lot of people were quite unhappy to see me replace Mr. Ness but they knew that Mitchell as senior partner would keep a rope on me but now they have nobody to protect their interests so they would rather see me out than having sole ownership of the firm. They'll come at me from every angle conceivable to man until enough time has passed that they're secure knowing that I'm not going to have chitlin bar-b-ques and revivals up in here. And they're going to come for you too. Believe me but it's nothing personal so don't take it personally. Chalk it up to change. People don't like change. They like routine, to know they're in control. Change puts them in a precarious position. Uncertainty is not comforting."

"A lot of it is racial as well," Samantha interjected.

"True but we can't look at it from that perspective. Getting caught up in racism and bigotry only clouds our sight and we have to stay focused on the task at hand and that's to stay focused on the business of making money for our clients."

"You're right. Damn, baby you see things so clearly. That's one of the reasons I love you so much she said grinning from ear-to-ear.

"Do one favor this week Sammy."

"What's that?"

"Just stay grounded and keep your eyes on the prize. Ignore all else."

"Aren't I always?"

"No doubt but I wasn't exactly sure we were on the same plane after we got so far off course this weekend. I'm just making sure we're on the same plane."

"After last weekend I don't think you'll ever have to worry about us being on a different page," Sam smiled before turning abruptly allowing him to see the deep split in her dress revealing a more than ample thigh.

"So we're here?" Anthony said pointing to his eyes and then hers.

"Yes sir. But I'd much rather be here," Sammy said pointing to his crotch and then hers. Both smiled as she opened the lobby door and headed back to her desk.

Anthony checked his watch and seeing he had a few minutes to spare headed for the elevator and outside to smoke.

"Mr. Pendleton?"

"Yes sir?"

"Detective Roberts. NYPD. Mind if I ask you a few questions?"

"Not at all if you don't mind going downstairs. I was just going outside to some."

"Not at all. Lead the way."

The two got off the elevator and headed for the street.

"Appreciate you stepping outside detective. Don't think it would have looked too good with potential investors wondering how stable the firm was following Mr. Mitchell's murder and a detective questioning the new CEO."

"So, now that you know why I'm here I guess we can forego all the small talk. With you to inherit the firm it just naturally follows that you would be the prime suspect."

"I understand that. Only one problem with your theory detective. I was in Baltimore at the time of Mr. Mitchell's untimely demise."

Detective pulled out a crumpled pack of cigarettes and lit one.

"Your alibi is tight Mr. Pendleton. Baltimore police have already confirmed that you were there with your pretty assistant, a Samantha King I believe."

Anthony was stunned. Samantha was in the room and out of plain sight when the Baltimore police questioned him. There was no way they could have known.

"And from what I understand you only paid for one room. Is that correct?"

Anthony dropped his head wondering what Sammy had to do with it or where the detective was going with this line of questioning.

"Am I to understand that you are married and your wife was unaware of your little liaison with Ms. King?"

"Yeah okay but what's the point?"

"The point is that although your alibi is airtight the fact remains that most people that plan or premeditate murder always have an airtight excuse. The fact remains that you more than anybody had probable cause to murder Mitchell. Now I'm going to ask you one time and one time only. Did you have anything to do with the murder of Mr. Mitchell?"

"And I'm going to tell you one time and one time only I had nothing to do with the murder of Mr. Mitchell."

"I'm going to give you the benefit of the doubt today Mr. Pendleton despite your meetings with Johnny Johnson better known as Duke a well-known Baltimore crime boss whose been indicted several times for murder. However, if I find that you are in any way connected with Mr. Mitchell's murder I'd suggest you have your lawyer on standby. Good day Mr. Pendleton."

Anthony was really shaken by the time Detective Roberts made his leave. It wasn't so much the fact that he'd met with Duke that bothered or even the fact he'd made allegations concerning his being with Sammy despite the fact that he was a married man. No it was the fact that he'd obviously been watched but whom and for how long? That was the real question, the real concern.

The board meeting went much as he'd expected and Anthony was at his best assuring everyone in attendance that he would stay the course and that there would be no major upheavals or chitlins served in the boardroom. That's what they wanted to hear and that's what he told them in attempts to placate their greatest fear. That a Black man was going to be in sole control of billions of dollars.

He'd play the role until all were secure and then and only after he had a majority share would he make the needed changes to take the firm to its true potential. But right now he like them was only interested in maintaining the status quo—well that was at least until... But for right now he had more pressing needs.

Returning to the office, he was surprised to find Samantha away from her desk while the phone rang incessantly.

"Anthony Pendleton. How may I help you?"

"What's up Blackman? I just read about Mr. Mitchell's murder. Thought that would have made you top dog Tone but I see they got you answering the phones. What's up with that? What happened? Did all them lily white motherfuckers run when they found out a nigga was in charge?" came the voice on the other end of the line followed by that booming laugh that could only be Malik.

"Damn baby, it's certainly good to hear from fam. This has got to be one of the worst days of my life."

"I kinda figured that. That's why I said I'd better call and see how my boy's doing. So, how are you farin' my brother?"

"I'm hanging in there as best I can despite all the shit going on."

"I know that's right. I've known you damn near all my life and I ain't never seen nothiin' really ruffle you. Even when we was young cats. Remember when we was trying to push up on those shorty's over there in Newark? How old was we then?"

"No more than fourteen or fifteen."

"Yeah, we was young. Remember that fine ass little skeezer that had your nose wide open. Oh, shit! What was her name? I can see her like it was yesterday. Cute little thing. Oh, what was her name?"

"Jackie. Yeah, Jackie Peoples. Remember we was sittin' up in her crib when her man came home?"

"Yeah," Anthony said reminiscing and showing every tooth in his head. "I thought it was her pops and it turned out to be her man. Nigga looked like he was thirty if he was a day."

"Nigga saw you sittin' there with his girl and pulled out a nine and you was cooler than a fan. I'm sayin' I remembered you looked dead at that nine and said 'nigga eitha you gonna use that shit or you not. If you not then me and my boy gotta bounce.' I was so proud of you that day I didn't know what to do. I said my nigga Ant is a fo' real 'g'. So I know if it anything short of lookin' down the barrel of a nine you gonna be alright."

Anthony laughed.

"This is a little different though. I went down to Baltimore last weekend and took Sammy with me and hung out with Duke a little and get back here and they're questioning me about Mitchell's murder and telling me that I'm the prime suspect."

"Well, that's to be expected."

"That is but the fact that they can tell me that Sammy was with me and that I've been hanging out with Duke is a little over the top."

"C'mon Tone. You know how the shit works. Nigga get too high or get too much power they gonna keep tabs on you. Ain't nobody immune. And you a nigga too risin' fast in an all White venue. What the hell you expect Blackman—a pat on the back and some words of encouragement? You lucky that's all they did.

"No, but I sure as hell didn't expect to be followed either."

"Count yourself as blessed Tone. And you fuckin' with that White girl you lucky they didn't string your Black ass up. You know what time it is."

"You right."

"But don't worry. I gotcha. Listen, I'm gonna put a couple of brothers around the house tonight so don't shoot nobody thinkin' they up to no good 'cause they hangin' 'round the crib," Malik laughed. "And first thing in the morning I'll start checkin' to see who's been following you. You stay easy and just run the firm. I'll take care of the rest."

"Thanks baby."

"Anything for you fam."

Anthony hung up the phone and went into the outer office only to see Sammy staring at the paper and looking as if she'd come face-to –face with the devil himself.

"What's wrong Samantha?" The cool Malik had just spoken of now a thing of the past.

Sammy turned to face him her face as white as a ghost as she handed him the newspaper. Taking the paper Anthony glanced to find whatever it was that had so unnerved the usually unflappable Samantha. Seeing the face he wondered if his face resembled hers as he reached out for the chair before falling back into it. What he saw was a small article but the picture under the caption said it all. **Convicted Felon Finally Meets Violent Fate**. Under the caption was a face he knew all too well. It read Joseph Assante known Mafia hit man was murdered gangland style in Bayside, Queens with two small caliber bullet wounds to the back of the head. First Mitchell and now Joe. It was all a bit too much for Anthony and too close to home. Glancing at Sammy he checked his watch. It was three-thirty and on a day such as this with all that was going he really should have stayed until at least seven or eight but instead he looked at Sammy.

"Samantha, hold all my calls. I'm leaving for the day."

"Are you okay?"

"Nothing that a good night's rest won't cure," he lied grabbing his coat and heading for the door.

"But Anthony you know you have Mr. Albright coming in at four and you're gonna need Albright."

"Just tell him I came down with something and reschedule him. Come on Sammy act like you know!"

And with that said Anthony Pendleton slammed the door behind him. Traffic was light and thirty minutes later he pulled up in the driveway of the modest three bedroom Tudor home and breathed a deep sigh of relief. Standing outside were two rather well dressed brothers. At first Anthony took them for detectives but when they spoke he realized that these were the gentlemen Malik had sent over and felt better still.

"Everything okay Mr. Pendleton?"

"Better just knowing you're here."

"Well, you can relax we have everything covered."

"Glad to hear that," Anthony said as he unlocked the door and made his way inside.

Inside all was quiet, almost too quiet. Making his way up to the bedroom Ant found Syl asleep and didn't bother to awake her. Always a light sleeper Sylvia turned and sat up abruptly.

"Oh Anthony I'm so sorry baby. What time is it anyway? I meant to have your dinner ready for you. I am so sorry. I must have dozed off."

"You're okay baby. I left work early. It's only a little after three."

"You left work early? Are you okay?"

Anthony laughed.

"Why does everyone keep asking me that? I told Sammy to reschedule all my appointments for this afternoon and she asked the same thing."

"Well, those of us that know Anthony Pendleton workaholic aren't used to this kind of behavior. So, how did it go?"

"You couldn't even imagine. Detectives asking questions, clients wanting to know the future of the firm, the board making sure that everything stays the course and bracing for the fallout which is sure to come and remember Joseph Assante the man Boots put into place to act as my bodyguard?"

"Yeah, what about him?"

"He's on the fourth page of the Daily News today. Took two behind the ear. Police are saying it was a hit."

"Some bodyguard," Syl said yawning.

"It's just crazy."

"Sounds like it. Listen why don't you just lie down. I'll bring you a drink and there're some movies on the nightstand. I stopped by Redbox on my way to the store this morning and picked up a couple. Why don't you just relax and take it easy for the rest of the day."

"I plan on it," Anthony said as he turned off his cell phone.

"Scotch and milk?"

"Sounds good."

"Okay. I'll be right back with your drink."

Anthony got up and was in the midst of getting undressed and showering when he heard the phone ring. Thinking it was his since she'd bought them matching phones for Christmas Anthony headed across the bedroom when he heard Syl.

"No, baby. He came home early and I'm pretty sure he's in for the evening so you can take the rest of the day off. Be back on the job first thing in the morning though."

"Yeah, I got the pictures. And believe me there's enough evidence right there to win on a case of infidelity but I'm greedy. I want the whole sh-bang, the whole kitten Kaboodle. So just be patient and go slow. You know the more I get the more your commission is."

"So you just want me to sit tight?"

"Yeah just keep doing what you're doing and who knows me or one of mine may end up with the whole firm."

Anthony was shocked. So, it was Syl that had had him followed and it was now obvious that she knew about his affair with Samantha but the real question was how much did she really know? Anthony turned on the shower and sat on the edge of the tub now lost in deep thought. If the day hadn't been excruciating enough now there were traitors in his own camp.

Taking an unusually long shower and letting the scalding hot water cascade down on his head he could feel the tension slowly ebb from his body. One thing was for sure he had to come up with a plan and he had to do it quick. But there was one thing that he had to do immediately and that was to get from under the same roof with Syl. He knew from past experiences that there was nothing like a woman's wrath and someone as cold and calculating as Syl only meant one thing. His life was in eminent danger.

A towel wrapped loosely around him he made his way out of the bathroom and proceeded to his side of the bed where he seeing the drink sipped long and slowly. Syl entered the room seconds later.

"Is it good?"

"C'mon! You know if you stuck your finger in it then it's on the money."

"Glad you like it," Syl said getting up and grabbing the movies. "You they finally had a copy of The Reader. Do you know how long I've been wanting to see it," she said sliding the movie in the DVD player. "I've heard so much about it that it'll probably be a let down now that I finally got it."

"Your expectations are probably too high."

"They always are and that's why people tend to get let down," she commented.

Anthony wondered if a double entendre was meant with the comment but chose to ignore it.

"I need to talk to you about something Syl."

"Can it wait 'til after the movie?"

"I suppose but you know you go to sleep every time you put a movie on."

"Not this time. Do you know how long I've waited to see it?"

"Okay but when it's over we need to talk."

"Okay Anthony," she said and it suddenly became very obvious to Anthony that he was now not the only one who'd considered their marriage a foregone conclusion.

Twenty minutes later Sylvia was asleep and to his surprise he found himself engrossed in the movie. Yet, despite the movies hold on him he had things to do. Dressing quickly he made his quickly to his car. The two men still held guard outside of his home and he nodded as he pulled away. The first thing he needed to do was to get in touch with Sammy. Afraid his phone may be tapped he texted her and told her to meet him at Macy's on 34th.

Parking in a garage, then doing his best to lose himself in the crowd on the way to Macy's he met Samantha in the men's cologne section.

"Thought you were calling it a day?"

"Listen Sam. I went home and overheard Syl talking to someone. She's the one that's been having me followed and told the police about us. I heard her telling someone that an infidelity case is a far cry from what she wants to do to me. She's talking about taking over the firm or something of that nature."

"Oh c'mon Ant. Sylvia doesn't know anything about trading or the such. Are you sure you're not being just a little bit paranoid."

"Paranoid hell. Sylvia's ex is the one that inspired me to head up my own firm. He was one of the first

Blacks in Georgia to open up his own minority firm. He has since opened in Charlotte, the banking capitol of the South and is doing quite well. Don't play her cheap. If she can't do it she has the connects and know how to get it done. She's smart, savvy, and vindictive. She's not the kind of person you want on your bad side."

"So, what do you think she's up to?"

"I wish I knew but what I do know is that you're going to take a leave of absence starting Wednesday. This is how you're going to do it. I want you to get a note from your doctor suggesting you begin your maternity leave immediately. I want you to go to Baltimore where I can have Duke look after you and John Hopkins is one of the best hospitals in the country so you'll be well cared for and that way if she decides to do anything stupid I'll have you out of harm's way. In the meantime, I'm going to suggest that I get an apartment in the city closer to the job just until I can get into the routine of being CEO and do everything to make Mitchell & Ness a success. In the meantime while the stock plummets in lieu of Mr. Mitchell's death I want you to buy all you can at those rates so instead of putting that two hundred thousand into a new firm we'll put our every dime into Mitchell & Ness and when it rises back to where it was prior to his death we will have made a killing and be majority shareholders to boot."

Samantha smiled.

"Sounds like a plan to me."

"In the meantime I'm going to study Syl like I study the NASDAQ until I get a feel for what she's trying to pull. Pack tonight and be ready to leave the following day. I don't know when I will see you again but you take care of Anthony Jr."

I was the first time he'd even made reference to the baby and it brought chills to her.

"I feel like I'm being put into the Witness Protection Program," Sammy said smiling but there were nothing but tears in her heart. "So, this is goodbye until?"

"Wish I could say when but I can't. Just know that I love you and please be safe and know that I'm coming for you."

Tears flowed and Anthony who now found himself on the verge as well turned and walked away but not before warning her that the phones may be tapped so text whenever possible.

Anthony then made his way down Broadway and stopped and picked up a throw away phone, bought enough minutes to last him a month and called Malik.

"What up Malik?"

"Same 'ol, same 'ol Blackman. What's good wit' you?"

"I wish I could call it but I can't. I'm working on your tail but so far nothing. What I do know is that there's a snitch in our midst. It's not the cops though but someone is definitely feeding them the skinny on your every action. My boy over in the 112 Precinct said he thinks it's a private dick by the name of Jake Roberts, a local boy out of Newark. He hasn't called to give me a definite on that but we're about ninety-nine and nine tenths sure that's who it is. I'm still waiting on his call. As soon as we find out who it is I'ma send a couple of outta town boys to rough him up a little bit and find out who he's working for. But on the real, the cops have all but cleared your name as far as 'ol man Mitchell but someone is feeding them dirt on you without they're asking. It's almost as if there's a conspiracy to bring you down."

"Who you telling? But you can call off your dog's my brother. I know who hired the private dick to tail me."

"Oh, you do. Mind sharing it with me. I bet it was one of those right there at Mitchell & Ness who don't want to see a Blackman make good."

"Wish it was that simple then I could better understand it but no, believe it or not it has nothing to do with the firm. It was Syl."

"Oh my God! Tell me you're lying."

"Wish I was. I left work early today and went home and overheard her on the phone."

"But why? Let me guess. The White girl?"

"You got it..."

"Damn Tone! I told you about that shit! You know what I think about that. You my boy and all but in all honesty I can't half blame her. Here you got this beautiful Black queen whose stood by you and supported you for the last ten or twelve years and watched you struggle to get where you are today and the minute you get there you dump her for some White chick."

"It ain't like that Malik. Me and Syl ain't hit it off in years. She consciously chose to ignore the fact that I wasn't feelin' her anymore. She was aware but decided that it was going to work because that's what she wanted."

"Ain't had nothin' to do with the fact that you already have a mother and that age is starting to catch up with her," Malik laughed.

"Fuck you man."

"Hey, but on the real didn't I tell you before you married her that you'll be coming into your prime and she'll be applyin' for AARP and social security?"

"You did."

"And now you're stuck with your cranky ass grandmother and she ain't playin'."

"That's about the size of it."

"So whatcha gonna do?"

'Well, I tried to keep up the marriage for appearances sake so that the clients would know that there's some stability within the firm but I think my only course of action is for us to separate."

"You think? That wife of yours is nothing to play with. Maybe I should increase the number of bodyguards."

Anthony laughed.

"Seriously though. You can't hold her off for a couple of weeks until the dust settles around Mr. Mitchell's death?"

"I'm going to try."

"And what about the White girl? You don't want another murder connected with Mitchell & Ness."

"I got her out of town and out of harm's way."

"Smart thinking. Damn if I had known all of this was going on I would have stationed Black and Tyree inside the house not out," Malik said chuckling again. "Listen Blackman I gotta go. Duty calls. I'll get with that dick just as soon as I get confirmation. I can take him off the case if you want me to."

"Let me think about it. I'll let you know the next time I talk to you."

Anthony knew how Malik worked, knew his methods and if you were in with him you couldn't ask for a more down brother but cross him and you'd bring down the wrath of Satan on you. Anthony was just glad Malik and he were like brothers. Now there was just one more thing that needed to be handled and a quick call to do would take care of that.

An hour or later he arrived home. The two men had now been relieved by two other men who looked equally as dangerous and Anthony chuckled as he thanked God he would never have to meet up with them one lonely night in a dark alley.

Syl snored heavily as he walked into the bedroom already changed into his pajamas just in case she were to wake up. He rewound the movie and watched no more than five minutes when he dozed off.

Somehow he felt alive and refreshed the next morning as he sat down at the breakfast table and looked at the two eggs before him. Sipping his orange juice he smiled at Syl he greeted him with a bubbly good morning.

"And how are you today Mrs. Pendleton?"

"Couldn't be better. I'm sorry I fell asleep on you last night. Don't know why I've been so tired lately."

"I'm sure it's that extra weight you've been lugging around lately," he said teasing knowing full well was overly conscious about her weight.

"Are you saying I'm getting fat?"

"You have put on a few pounds."

"I guess so smartass. I am eating for two you know," she said almost remorsefully.

"Ah baby, you could add fifty and you'd still look good to me. After all if I had been marrying for looks I damn sure would have married somebody else," he said chuckling.

"Screw you Anthony. You certainly know how to make a girl feel good."

"Thougt I was complimenting you."

"Compliment hell. Don't you know this is when a girl is at her most vulnerable? When she's pregnant she feels like no man in the world wants her. She's not sexy and everyone knows she's been active and half the time the man doesn't want to be seen with her."

"Ah, come on baby you know that's not true."

"Oh no well let me ask you this then. When's the last time you asked me out to dinner. I know one thing. You haven't asked me since I've been pregnant. Half the time I feel as if you're ashamed of me and just want to keep me locked up in this dungeon forever."

Anthony could only smile. So caught up in the playful banter he almost forgot that this very same woman was the one having him followed and was so intent on making his life from here on out a living hell. And if no one else he knew she was quite capable of bringing him all the way down to his knees. He was only glad he'd come to know in time.

"Tell you what baby. I want you dressed in your finest maternity dress and I mean one that accentuates that bubble where there used to be abs and be ready to go at six o'clock sharp."

"And why is that? You plan on taking me somewhere on the outskirts of Eden where nobody'll see or recognize me or now that I'm your wife."

Anthony chuckled again.

"No, baby. I'm planning on taking you anywhere your little heart desires. As long as it's posh and the food is plentiful and my baby's happy."

"Oh, baby. That's the Anthony Pendleton I used to know before..." Syl blurted out before stopping short.

"Before what?"

"Oh nothing. Just thinking out loud."

I'm sure Anthony thought wiping his mouth and getting up from the table.

"Let me get out of here."

Chapter 10

Arriving at the offices of Mitchell & Ness Anthony thought about Sylvia for the first time in a very long time. She was a good woman who only wanted what most women wanted and that was no more than a faithful and loving husband. And up until a few months ago he'd taken pride in being just that. He didn't know what had cause d the change in him. It certainly wasn't Sammy. She'd been with him seven long years and in all that time he'd never even approached her. No, it was something within their marriage or a lack thereof and as much as he could feel her love, exuberance and warmth where he was concerned he no longer could reciprocate in kind. He'd felt closer to her this morning than he had in a long time but he knew there was no going back. He loved her. There was no doubt about that but the question was was he in love with her and to that came a resounding no.

"Morning Mr. Pendleton," came Sammy's voice as he strode across the lobby and into his office.

Why was she here? He'd ask her to get her self together to leave and yet here she was as if he'd said nothing. He'd hate to have her fired and escorted from the building but if she didn't understand the danger she was in he certainly did. He knew bits and pieces of Sylvia's past and cared to know no more but one thing was for sure those that somehow incurred her wrath always seemed to come up on the short end of the stick. He hated to see it happen to Sammy but that was a sure bet if she didn't find a way to make herself scarce.

Anthony entered his office and found his desk a hodge-podge of papers which he immediately began sorting through but not before pushing the button on the intercom and summoning Samantha.

"Ms. King may I see you in my office please?"

"On my way Mr. Pendleton."

Sammy walked in wearing a black suit. The single breasted jacket that at one time hung loosely was now snug and Sammy had purposely omitted not worn the black camisole which though sexy partially covered her more than ample breasts. And despite her accusing Anthony of trying to fatten her up so she could have the thighs and hips of Black women she was very well-endowed in that area as well and if she had tried to cover them in her attempts at office decorum all that seemed to take a back seat today.

It was obvious she wore no underclothes and on closer look Anthony was at a loss for words.

"Close the door behind you Sammy."

Doing as she was told she closed the door and locked it.

"Yes sir, Mr. Pendleton. What can I do for you?"

Still mesmerized but the woman's beauty he wondered if she were thinking what he was. Gathering his thoughts Anthony at last managed to speak.

"Sammy, perhaps I didn't express the danger we're in right through here."

"I believe you expressed yourself quite clearly Anthony," she said smiling and at the same time lifting her dress to reveal her pubic hairs which were wet and matted. "But it seemed such a cold way to leave the man I love and then that part about not knowing when the next time you'd see me didn't exactly sit well with me. So, I started thinking about a role reversal. You see within the confines of Mitchell & Ness you may be my supervisor but aside from that you're my lover and soon to be my child's father and for some reason I just didn't feel the love in our little discourse last night. Now I know you're under an exorbitant amount of stress but I just feel that you need to make some concessions on your demands. So, let's do a little role reversal right through here. Get up and let me sit down," Sammy said rather adamantly.

"Oh, you're the boss now huh."

"Just get up."

Anthony stood up and Sammy sat down.

"I guess you have a few directives and I would mind carrying them out but I'm swamped in work. I don't even know why you want to play games at this point in time."

"Kneel down and shut up Anthony. Your next appointment isn't until ten and its eight thirty. So be a good fellow and just do as you're told. Now come here," Samantha pulled the dress up 'til she had it bunched around her mid-section. Sliding down in the captain's chair and revealing all of her goodies she beckoned Anthony.

"I want you to eat it like it's the last supper baby. I want you to leave me raw and sore so I'll remember you for weeks after."

Kneeling down in front of her Anthony proceeded to do as he was told despite her screams for him to stop. When he finally did she'd come at least four times and was drenched and shaking.

"Think you'll remember daddy now?"

Too exhausted to answer Samantha nodded her head but Anthony was hardly finished. Standing now she hardly noticed Anthony unbuckled his belt and let trousers fall to his feet. Erect he lifted her legs to his shoulders and drove his manhood deeply into her.

Semi-conscious Samantha moaned with each thrust which proved deeper and harder than the one before.

"Oh my God Anthony! What are you trying to do to me?!?!" she yelled in between screams.

"You said you wanted something to remember me by."

"Please Anthony you're hurting me."

But there was no stopping him now as he let go of all the demons and frustrations that he'd inherited in the past weeks. And then just as suddenly as it had started it was over. Sammy was no longer conscious having passed out after the last orgasm. Anthony picked the unconscious woman up and placed her on the sofa in his office and let her sleep for an hour or so before waking her. Promising to see her before the week was out Sammy gathered herself and resigned herself to her new life.

Baltimore wouldn't have been her first choice but with Duke affording her all the amenities possible and Anthony constantly showering her with gifts it was bearable. And anytime she had a hankering for her man all she had to do was pick up the phone. Anthony would take an early lunch catch a quick flight and be there in forty-five minutes and be home for dinner. But after a month or two the gifts were not enough and the visits fewer still. Duke had allocated his youngest son Trey as Miss Sammy's fulltime driver and over the months they became quite close. Samantha , not knowing anyone in the area confided in Trey and when she became dismayed and distraught by her plight it was Trey who got the brunt of her dismay.

"Let me ask you something Trey."

"Go ahead Samantha ask away."

"Okay. Let's just say you were in love with a woman who lived in a different city and I mean you really, really loved this girl. Wouldn't you make every effort to see her and to be with her?"

"Yeah, I suppose I would."

"And if you didn't what kind of impression would that girl get?"

"I guess she'd think that I didn't love her as much as I said I did."

"And why pray tell would she think that?"

"Because I'm not making every effort to see her."

Samantha had heard enough. She'd gotten the answers she needed and they concurred with her own thinking. Truth of the matter was she was no better than his mistress, his concubine, who was to bear his child. He'd played her, taken everything she had to offer and when things became a bit too complicated at home he'd shipped her off. Oh, sure he'd fly down to tap that ass every now and then but as of late she wasn't even worth the flight down to see her. To make matters worse it had been close to two weeks since he'd called her. But she wasn't one to be used and discarded like some old rug or piece of trash. No, he would pay. Nobody rode this road without paying the toll. And Anthony Pendleton was going to pay. She knew too much and had too much dirt on him for him to walk away Scott free.

"Hello."

"Hey baby boy. This is Duke."

"Hey Duke baby how are you?"

"Oh I'm doing pretty good for an old man. Listen, the reason I'm calling you is about Samantha."

"Yeah, I've meaning to call her but I've just been so swamped. How is she anyway?"

"Well, health wise she's great. Been seeing her primary care physician on the regular and he says she's doing well. You know I allocated my youngest son as her driver and they've become pretty close over the last couple of months."

"So what are you saying Duke?"

"Well, Sammy has grown pretty close to Trey and tells him everything and right now she feels as if she's been abandoned which is normal for a woman in her position. Says you haven't been to see her or called her in weeks. To make a long story short she's a little distraught and says that she's not gonna take this shit any longer. Says she has too much shit on you to let you just walk away. Says you're going to feel her pain."

"Ah c'mon Duke that's just a woman scorned talking. Nothing to come of it."

"I hear you and believe me I understand but you know should she start talking we'd all go down. All I can say is that you'd better be damn glad that I heard it and not someone else. If someone, say Boots were to have heard that chances are she'd already be dead. So, to be on the safe side I think you'd better get her out of here with the quickness and put a muzzle on her."

"I hear you Duke. I'll handle it."

"I'm just telling you 'cause I know you have feelings for the woman and I know she's carrying your child."

"Good look Duke. I appreciate it. I'll have her out of there first thing in the morning. Let me call her now."

"Okay Anthony. Let me know how things work out."

"I'll do that and thanks for the heads up."

No, sooner had he hung up the phone than he dialed Samantha's number.

"What's up baby?"

"Well, nice of you to call."

"Hey Sammy," Anthony began only to be cut off in mid-stream.

"Don't hey Sammy me. You could have at least had the decency to call and see how the mother of your baby's doing or better yet to see how your baby's doing. It's been over two weeks since I've heard from you and every time I call the damn thing goes to voicemail. What's the point of having a phone if you're not going to bother to turn it on?"

"Are you finished?"

"Yeah, in fact I'm not really sure I have anything at all to say to you."

"Listen Sammy."

"I know you've been busy and under unbelievable pressure since Mr. Mitchell was murdered. I know. I know. I know. I've rehearsed your lines a thousand times over and over in my head and how you always need me by your side and you're going through the same withdrawal as badly as I am and this thing would make a dope fiend going cold turkey think he was on a cruise to Club Med. Or that I'm here for my own good and my protection but the truth of the matter is that I'd risk everything just to be with you. Only fucking problem with that is is that the man or at least who I once considered my man doesn't feel the same and has shipped me who the fuck knows where and seems okay abandoning me somewhere where I don't know anyone for as he calls it my own protection. Ain't that some shit. And he ain't even got the decency to pick up the fuckin' phone and say how are you doin'. This is a man that doesn't forget to send the bicycle courier he ain't seen in a month a fuckin' Christmas gift but he can't remember the woman where he stuck his dick last. Ain't that some bullshit?''

"Are you finished? If you've said what you had to say let me know so I can say what I have to say."

"Go ahead player. Run you're your smooth shit and see what affect it has. I'm done. On the real Ant, you're wasting your time."

"Okay, I understand that you may be done. And I can certainly understand why you feel that way. For me not to call was an obvious blunder. What can I say? I fucked up baby? But I have a good reason if you can wrap your brain around that for a minute."

"There is no excuse Anthony. None whatsoever."

"Can I finish?"

"Go the fuck on."

"Baby, I go to work every day and believe you me things have changed. I mean with Mitchell gone is one thing. He didn't do but so much so his end isn't very hard to handle. I can carry his responsibilities as well as my own with very little problem. But with you gone it's a totally different scenario. A good deal of the time you carried me. Now instead of that happening I have to carry Mitchell's load as well as yours and train a temp at the same time. And Lord knows where they get these temps from but they are the pits. Had one who used to sing the alphabet out loud to make sure the letters were in the right order before filing anything. Then along with work I have to worry about my baby and how she's doing so I came up with a plan a couple of weeks ago after meeting with Johnathan Dalton."

"The real estate tycoon?" Sammy said in awe. "I just saw him on CNN or was it Face the Nation. He's sharp. The man knows his way around the real estate market."

"Or so it seems."

"And what is that supposed to mean?"

"Well, from what he tells me he's taking a beating right through here. Even the rich and the famous are playing it pretty close to the vest. They're not buying like they used to and so his monies are tied up and he's being strangled like everyone else. Right now he has some homes—and I mean some beautiful homes—that he's trying to liquidate and just break even. He's trying to diversify and get his feet wet in the market."

"And what's that have to do with you not being able to pick up the phone."

"It has everything in the world with me not being able to pick up the phone."

"Hurry up and finish Anthony I have more interesting things to do than to listen to your bullshit.

"I'm trying to if you would stop interrupting and let me finish. You see Syl's called off the dogs and everything's pretty good on the home front. In fact, tonight is the night I tell her that I'm leaving her and want a divorce. But anyway truth of the matter is I miss you so much. How does Sade say it? 'Like the desert misses the rain' so every night for the past two weeks I've been leaving work and going out on the island and home shopping. I've been to Wyandanch, Montauk Point, the Hampton's... I mean I've been everywhere trying to find a home for my baby. I wanted to surprise you but even though they're nice I just don't know if you'd be happy with them."

"Oh my God! Anthony! I don't know if you're serious but damn you do know how to get to a girl."

"You don't know if I'm serious?" Anthony laughed. "Just look down at third finger left hand."

Caught off guard Samantha looked down at the four carats and smiled.

"So what's the verdict?"

"Well by the time I get back over to Jersey it's somewhere in the neighborhood of eleven or twelve o'clock and I just crash."

"No, I meant the verdict on the house?"

Anthony laughed.

"I know what you meant. I decided that we'll look together and you can make the decision but in the meantime I got us a loft on the lower eastside in Soho. Runs about two and a half mil a year but like I said Dalton's in dire straits so he let me have it for nine hundred and fifty thousand a year. It's a steal. And I had an interior decorator come in and do it up right. But like I said it's only temporary 'til you pick out a home. I got you a plane reservation on American Airlines for nine a.m. tomorrow morning and Duke's got some men that are going to move your stuff and bring it up here by the weekend."

There was silence and Anthony smiled knowing that he'd just blown her away and she was probably crying on the other end. He thought about rubbing it in and the problem with jumping the gun and assuming all the time and then decided to apologize but realized that an apology on his part would just be rubbing it in and so he thought he would get off and just let her keep dwell on her bad assumptions. Besides he had much more pressing matters at hand. It was finally time to break the news to Syl.

"Your mother's going to pick you up at Newark Airport at ten forty-five tomorrow morning and swing by your apartment so you can pick up any valuables. The movers will be moving the remainder of your stuff and it should be in the new place by the weekend.

"Is there anything you missed?" Samantha asked, the tone of her voice revealing the tears she hid.

"Aside from missing you—no—I don't think I did. But let me go. I have to go home and break the news to Syl."

"Be safe."

"I always am."

A half an hour later Anthony stood in the living room of 1401 Woodcrest Lane. The house was quiet aside from the muted sounds of Kem emerging from the master bedroom. Anthony thought about what lay ahead and poured a double shot of Patron and had a seat on the living room sofa before picking up the remote and putting on Coltrane's Ballads and letting the Patron do its job. He considered the best way to approach Syl and after mulling over the situation for some time realized that there was no easy way to tell a woman that their marriage was over and especially a woman who was as deeply in love as Sylvia was. And so draining the last of the Patron he made his way upstairs to have a final meeting with Syl.

"Hey baby. I must have dozed off. I didn't hear you come in. You been here long?"

"No. I just walked in."

"So, how was your day? You must be starved let me run down and throw something together. You feel like spaghetti?"

"Nothing for me Syl. I think we need to talk."

"About what love?"

"There's no need to beat around the bush or sugarcoat it."

"Sugarcoat what, sweetheart?"

"Sylvia, I want a divorce."

Sylvia paused for a second before reaching for her cigarettes on the nightstand.

"Excuse me. Could you bother repeating that because I know I didn't hear you right? Would you repeat that?"

"Listen Syl. I've thought about this long and hard and given it considerable thought and I'm not happy. In fact I can't remember the last time I've been happy and with all the shit I've got on me when I step out of this house the least I can ask when I come home at night is to be happy in the confines of my own home and I'm not."

"Is that it?"

"That's it in the nutshell."

Sylvia drew long and hard on her cigarette before speaking.

"You know it's funny but I kind of suspected something like this ever since I got back from mama's. Call it women's intuition. Call it what you want but I knew something was amiss. But tell me this. Why after seven years did you see fit to sleep with Sammy? You were my pride and joy Anthony. When all my girlfriends were calling me crying or relating some story about their men or men they knew who were cheating on their wives I held you up on a pedestal. You were the crown jewel. You were every woman's knight in shining armor. And I toasted and touted you as being the ideal man—loyal, faithful—and in love. Why after seven years?"

"First of all, Sammy has worked for me for seven years and you're right. For seven years we kept it purely professional but Sammy was not the reason. Sammy was the result. She had nothing to do with the cause. If everything were perfect at home I might never have recognized Sammy at all. But things weren't right at home and so I looked around for something or someone to alleviate my pain and she was there."

"So, and with all I do for you and our marriage to keep it knew and wonderful you're trying to tell me that you're in pain and unhappy? Well, I'll be damned. But I guess if that's where you are what can I say? I really don't know what to tell you. So, what's your plan and what do you plan on doing concerning your child?"

"Well, with all the added work and responsibility I was planning on getting a place closer to the office and just concentrate on work for a while and see what happens."

"That sounds like a plan. Might give you time to think and appreciate your wife of twelve years. What did Carole King say in Big Yellow Taxi? 'Hey it only goes to show that you don't know what you got' til it's gone. They paved paradise and put up a parking lot.' Hopefully you'll figure it out sooner than later. I'll give you a month and I'm sure you'll be back. If you're not and still feel like this is truly what you want to do I promise you a divorce like you've never seen before?" Syl smiled. "But I'm not worried after twelve years of me being at your beck and call I think you'd be hard pressed to find another woman as sharp and adept at being a wife than I am s I have all the confidence in the world that my baby will be back and a better man for the time he went away and had a chance to appreciate me. So when are you leaving?"

"After that little speech I'm ready to leave now."

"That's your guilt sweetheart? But I understand. You'll come to your senses in about a month if it takes that long. A lot of men go through it. It's natural. I call it menopause and you'll survive. But I will tell you this. If I even think that you're shacking up or seeing somebody Anthony there will be hell to pay. Do you understand me?"

"See! That's what I'm talking about Syl. I don't need another mother. I need a wife. I don't need someone who's going to chastise and punish me when I do something they don't approve of. I have the right to exercise my own free will. I haven't done anything to be confined to the prison of your insecurities."

"My insecurities? I know you're not serious! Motherfucker, I should be all in your ass right now. If I have insecurities they come from the fact that I've given you twelve of the best years of my life and while your ass is out there sleeping with some White bitch that couldn't wipe my ass if her name was Scott Tissue. You go ahead and do some dumb shit and see what the fuck happens. Now get the fuck out. Go and get yourself together and don't say shit to me until you're ready to make some amends for your fucked up behavior."

Anthony grabbed a few of his things and threw them in a bag and headed for the door but not before grabbing the bottle of Patron. Liquor stores were closed this time of night and he didn't much feel like the company of some drunk in a bar. Heading into the Lincoln Tunnel he took a long swig from the bottle and thought about Syl's words and immediately dismissed them. He felt little or no remorse and was glad in fact to put that chapter of his life behind him. The loft was like he said close to work and a welcome change from the commute to Jersey every night. It had never been his idea to move to Jersey in the first place. It had been Syl's wish and so like everything else he'd gone along with it but he'd always loved the smell of urine in the subway and the smell of garbage walking down the streets on sweltering summer days. He loved the Jamaican music blaring from the Jamaican restaurants and the constant bustle that made New York the big apple. And he was more than a little happy to be returning to all that he knew that was life and good. He only hoped that Sammy shared his sentiment and chose to remain in the city. The thought of Sammy coming home tomorrow made him smile even more and he was glad that one chapter of his life was over and another just beginning.

Chapter 11

"Oh my God! Baby I am so glad to be home. You know Baltimore's a wonderful city but there ain't nothing like New York. Damn! It feels so good to be home," Sammy said the exuberance spilling over and oozing through the phone.

"And it sure is good to hear your voice." Anthony replied with enough exuberance to match hers. Feels like it's been years since I talked to you even though it was only last night."

"Who are you telling? I can't wait to see you."

"Where are you?"

"Downstairs in the lobby."

"Well, why are you calling me? Come on up."

"Didn't think that would be a good idea the way I feel."

"And how do you feel?" Anthony asked as he grabbed his keys and headed for the door."

"Feel like I'd jump on you and give you the biggest hug and kiss and somehow I don't think that would go over too big in front of the clients."

"You right. I'm on my way."

"Thought you'd be here by now."

"Can't move any faster love."

Minutes later Anthony exited the elevator and there she was. Standing looking better than she had in the seven years that Anthony had known her. If there had been; there was little or no doubt who the next Mrs. Anthony Pendleton would be. Hugging her but as not to be too passionate in lieu of onlookers Anthony whispered to her.

"Let's head out so I can hold you the way I've been dreaming of for the last three weeks."

Together they walked side-by-side each trying to get a word in as they clamored on about this and that and how they'd missed each other like the desert missed the rain for blocks on end until Samantha a little weary from walking stopped suddenly.

"Where are you taking me?" she asked abruptly."

"Anywhere you want to go. Let's grab a cup of coffee at the corner café and catch up on things," she suggested.

"There are some other things I'd rather catch up on," he said winking.

"I so want that to happen but I have a meeting in about forty minutes. Can I get a rain check for say this evening?"

"I guess so if that's the best I can do," Samantha pouted.

"I promise I'll make it worth your while."

"And you can best believe I'm gonna hold you to that Mr. Pendleton."

"Well, until this evening then... let me grab you to a cab. Here's the key and address for the loft. Call me as soon as you give it the once over and let me know if it's just a temporary residence or if you'd like to spend the rest of your life there," Anthony said smiling and kissing the woman on the cheek as he opened the cab door for her.

"I'll call you as soon as I get settled."

"I'll be looking for your call," Anthony said closing the door to the taxi. Staring at the cab as it pulled out into traffic Anthony grinned.

"Damn, I am one lucky man."

Samantha entered the loft and was shocked by the sheer size. It was huge and she had to admit that all her reservations about pipes hanging from the ceiling and how it would her months to decorate had all been for naught. Exquisitely decorated she saw no reason to change a thing and if she hadn't known she knew now that Anthony loved her. Off from the master bedroom was a walk-in closet already outfitted with at least a hundred pair of shoes and a wardrobe that was not only expensive but tasteful and chic. The bar and refrigerator were well stocked and it was apparent that he'd spent the last three months making sure everything was perfect. Sammy laid across the king sized canopied bed closed her eyes and wondered how it could possibly get any better than this. She awoke to the sounds of the elevator doors open and was surprised to find Anthony home so early.

"Oh, sweetie it is so good to see you. You're home early. What time is it?"

"It's six thirty baby."

"Oh my. I must have lost track of time," Samantha said yawning.

"You never called me to tell me what you thought of the place so I take it that you aren't really feeling it."

"Are you serious? I love it. You know it's always been my dream to live in Manhattan, right in the center of things, and yet be able to close the world out should I choose to. So, if I could have chosen my dream house this would no doubt be it. And did you see the kitchen? It's a girl's dream," Samantha went on and on about the house, the clothes and Anthony knew that he had hit pay dirt. "You know a lot of people don't like the city but I am not one of those people—maybe when I'm seventy or eighty—but I love the fact that it's alive and everything's accessible. I mean if I want a pastrami and Swiss at three in the morning or want to hear some jazz it's all within a couple of blocks. I love that. How could you not love New York? Everything's so convenient."

"My sentiments exactly," Anthony smiled happy to know that she was pleased but happier with the fact that they were on the same page. He'd attempted to share the same sentiment with Syl but growing up in the country she was vehemently opposed to living in the city referring to it on more than one occasion as overwhelming. God how relieved he was to get away her. But never mind the bad memories he had too much ahead of him.

It was Friday and Anthony was only too happy he didn't have to get up the next day after talking and making love until the wee hours of the morning. By the time he returned on Monday all was back to normal and he ventured he could not have asked for anything better. They'd both chosen to stay at home and just enjoy each other's company and they'd done just that with no apprehension or reservation. And they talked about everything from the goings on at Mitchell & Ness to picking out names for the baby and where they were going to enroll Anthony Jr. in school.

The days and weeks passed much in the same manner and whereas Syl hated losing her shape Samantha seemed to adore the inches and pounds she was adding. Never had she been this happy and Anthony was the reason. She'd invested every dime she had and even went so far as to have her mother liquidate her 401K and invest as well and in a little over a six month period had tripled both their investments in Mitchell & Ness and was now counting the dividends and contemplating selling houses after finding out what the loft was worth.

Anthony's spirits picked up as well. He somehow felt freer and more alive even with the added responsibilities of being the CEO and primary stockholder in Mitchell & Ness. No longer was he clocked by a jealous wife and when he went out at night to network or just throw down a few beers with the boys he didn't feel compelled to call in and state his whereabouts but then why would he? He would have had to be a fool to do anything to jeopardize his relationship with Sammy and only prayed that he felt the same way in twenty years as he did now.

All was well but Anthony had an uneasy feeling that began to grow . At first, he thought he was being paranoid but then he realized Syl had hired a private detective in the past and the way she'd dismissed had never set comfortably with him. The Syl he knew would go down in a bloody heap still ranting and raving until her last breath should she even think someone had done her an injustice so for her to let him walk away with barely a whimper was quite out of character. So caught up in his new found freedom he had never stopped to look back but it was going on a month and a half and the fact that she hadn't called to scream or yell or even check up on him unnerved Anthony more than a little. And the fact that he always felt like someone was peering over his shoulder nowadays didn't lessen his mounting apprehension.

"Doesn't it appear strange to you that we haven't heard anything from Syl Ant?"

He heard her but did not respond at once. He'd had the same thoughts over the past week only compounded the thought of someone following him constantly. It had started to become unnerving and yet he didn't want to make too much of it or blow it out of proportion but since she'd brought it up he should at least share his feelings on the subject with her but not enough to upset or alarm her.

"You know it's funny you bring that up Sammy," Anthony said putting down the copy of Sports Illustrated he was reading. "I didn't want to alarm you 'cause I may just be a little paranoid. But I swear I feel like someone's following me and the last time I had this feeling Syl had put a private detective on me. Well, I was sure he was out of the picture but I feel the same way I did then only I don't have any proof."

"You honestly think she would try that again?"

"To be honest I don't know how far Syl would go but for her to be this quiet is not right. It's not right at all."

"Why don't you call her? That way you'd at least get a better feel for where her head is at."

"I said I was curious I didn't say I was crazy," he laughed. "But I am surprised I haven't heard from her by now. When I was leaving she gave me a month to get my head right and warned me about seeing another woman but maybe she's come to her senses."

Samantha and Anthony thought about what he'd just said and then said 'nah' in unison and fell into each other's arm tickled that they had the same thought.

"But you know Ant. In a way I wish she'd come on and bring so it would be over once and for all."

"And trust me Sylvia knows that we can never have total peace until she's out of the way and believe she's in no rush to make a move. For her it's like playing chess. Each move has to be deliberate and well thought out. Right now she has us in a quandary, sorta like having s in check so she's sitting pretty but I'm telling you Sam she knows our every move. She's a sick puppy and she's watching everything we do. She's just waiting for an opportunity to strike and to see how painful she can make it."

"Oh, Anthony stop tryin' to make her out to be some sort of monster," Samantha said sarcastically.

"I've seen her in action Sammy and it ain't nothin' pretty. And that's real talk. You just be care and lay low 'til this whole thing blows over."

"What else can I do?" Sammy replied rubbing her stomach.

The doctor had recommended bed rest for the duration of her pregnancy and Anthony was more than a little happy about this. He could more easily eye on her than if she were allowed to go traipsing around the city and being in the house kept her out of harm's way. And Lord knows what Syl was conspiring.

Samantha's concurrence with Anthony only heightened his awareness when it came to Syl and all those weeks he'd relegated her to a mere memory in lieu of better times came cascading down upon him a few days later at work. Returning from a painstaking meeting with the board who though in absolute agreement with revenues and the third quarter earnings were somehow still deadpanned against the changes made by Anthony within the company. Sitting at his office trying to figure out what it was they were so opposed to Miriam the cute little temp buzzed the intercom.

"Call on line one from a Mr. Malik for you Mr. Pendleton."

"Thanks Miriam," he said before picking up the phone.

"What's good Blackman?"

"Same ol' same 'ol. Yo, listen Tone. You know the private detective Syl hired a couple of months ago that was feeding the police dirt on Syl's behalf?"

"Yeah well you know some of the boys and I met with him and convinced him that working on Syl's behalf might not be in his best interest. You know the boys can be rather convincing. Anyway Jake came around and turned out to be a rather good person to have on the payroll. But you know he probably isn't as shrewd as he could be and so I had him going back selling Syl a line and I kinda think my man overdid it. When he was finished he had you rather for canonization to be a saint and you know Syl wasn't going for that. So, about a month and a half ago she fired him saying there was no longer any need for his services. But from what he was telling me she must have someone else o the case as well because he said that she knew all about Samantha leaving the firm."

"Is that right? Funny thing, but I was telling Sammy just last weekend that I believe I was being followed. Just had that feeling. I was just telling her that."

"Well, if you'd let me finish I can probably clear all your little premonitions up. You see you might not be too far off the beaten path. You know private detectives are like cops. They all have their little fraternities and it seems when she fired 'ol Jake she hired one of his buddies to replace him and they're pretty close so he comes and tells me that you're not off the hook yet and you're still being tailed. Jake is supposed to meet with the guy tonight for drinks and give him the same option I gave him. If need be I'll put him on retainer and give him a little more than Syl but truth be told the woman's not only relentless but has some mighty deep pockets as well. I won't even tell you what she pays these toy cops a day. It would make you cringe."

"You right don't tell me but you know Syl came to the marriage with her own money. I never asked any questions but she has money. You know William Stanton?"

"The stock market tycoon out of Charlotte?"

"The very same."

"Yeah what about him?"

"That was her first husband and he paid alimony after their divorce in excess of twenty five thousand a month and still pays and she's been married twice since."

"Get outta here?!?!"

"And from what I understand her second husband, a local boy where she grew up built a construction that's still up and running. She's the sole proprietor and it has assets somewhere in the neighborhood of about four million."

"Are you serious Tone."

"Dead! You know a few months ago when I was trying to solicit the funding to open my own firm Syl took a trip down to North Carolina and stayed a total of three or four days and came back with two million in cold cash to be used as startup capital. I never asked her to."

"And you're giving up the goose that lays the golden eggs for what? For a cute ass and a smile. Tone, my brother, have you lost your fuckin' mind?"

Anthony had to laugh.

"I've always believed you have to stay true to yourself and whereas money may very well be the key to your happiness Malik it is only a means to an end. To be honest with you I'd be satisfied with a flat some good music, some nice wine and some good conversation. Doesn't take a lot my brother," Anthony said laughing again.

"That is true but see you never grew on jam sandwiches where you jam two pieces of bread together and pretend there's something in the middle. And I gotta admit I've never seen you happier than the last couple of months shacked up with Princess Di. So, maybe money isn't the answer for everyone and as long as you keep that perspective and keep those shares rising up the Dow I'll agree with everything you say," Malik kidded. "And if it takes a White girl to keep my boy smiling and finding new ways to make money for his friends then I'm turning in my lifelong membership to the cause and going out and try to find me one too."

Both men laughed

"I'll let you know how tonight turns out between Jake and his boy but on the real even if he goes along with our proposition chances are she'll simply hire someone else. I'm telling you she's relentless. You crossed her and she's not going to end this until she sees you in as much pain as she's in. You can mark my words."

"Sad but true. I just hope that you're wrong."

"You and me both. You just be careful. Women can be treacherous."

"Don't I know."

Rapping to Malik always made Anthony feel a certain kind of way. He was one of the few people that

Anthony could really be himself with without worrying about how he came across. It was what it was. There were no double entendre or innuendos. Like it or not Malik put it out there and you could either chew and swallow it or choke and throw up on it. But he laid it out there plain for your consumption. It was so different from his clients with their fixation on words and double talk. Even the women he knew demanded a certain gene se qua that wouldn't allow him to be free and easy in his own right. That was except for Syl who was well educated but knew that alone behind closed doors she could let her hair down and allowed him to do so as well. They'd grown up in different but had obviously gone to the same school of hard knocks. And perhaps that's why he feared her now. They were two of the same. It wasn't about retribution and getting even so much as being one up. If you hurt me I may have to kill you and suffer the repercussions later. He'd always liked that in her and often had to temper the flame but that was when the win at all costs was directed at someone else. But now it was directed at him and as Malik commented, she was if nothing else relentless.

Perhaps Sammy had been right. Maybe he should call her and see if he couldn't call off the attack before it got out of hand and Lord knows what her intent was or who it was directed at. Well, he knew it was directed at him butshe was type to leave him standing so he could agonize watching his troops fall all around him.

"Syl. Hey how are you?"

"I'm good and you Anthony?"

"I'm well. Busy as usual but I can't complain."

"I'm sure you are. You've gotten everything you wanted. You're single living in Manhattan and running one if not the top firm on Wall Street. What more could you ask for? How many brothers out there would die to be in your position?"

"You right but if you don't have someone to love all of that doesn't matter much now does it?"

Anthony threw it out there and wondered if she would bite.

"Is that right?" she asked rather rhetorically stealing his favorite line.

"That's what they tell me. But I thought maybe you could shed a little insight on that for me."

"Being coy is not your strong suit Anthony. If there's something you want to know just ask me."

"In all honesty all I really wanted to know where you were as far as I was concerned."

"Why is that important to you? You left here close to two months ago and this is the first time I've heard from you in that entire time. And out of the clear blue you want to call me and ask where we are and how

I've compartmentalized my marriage and love for you. Wow! Can I ask you a question?"

"Sure Syl, anything?"

"What brought this on?"

"I'm just curious."

"Curious or apprehensive," she smirked.

"Maybe a little of both."

"Don't be Anthony. It's not up to me to judge and pass sentence on you. So, if you're worried about suffering any repercussions from your actions it won't be me that brings the wrath upon you. But then again if you feel righteous in your actions then this conversation is pointless. All I can say is that I hope that you Sammy and the baby are happy. I wish you the best. I really do," and with that Anthony heard the phone go dead.

He was too in shock to be relieved but couldn't wait to get home and have a sit down with Sammy and try to decipher the discourse and see how much was rhetoric and what part truth.

Chapter 12

"Hey mommy."

"Hey Papi," Samantha replied kissing Anthony. "And how was your day lover.

"More of the same. You know, meeting with clients to assure them that we're taking a slightly more aggressive approach but we're still on course."

"Are they receptive?"

"For the most part. They may not believe or understand the strategy but then they're neither buying the concept or the strategy they're buying the man selling it. For the most part they're buying me which is why it's so important to appear to be ultra-conservative in this business. You might take chances with their food or their religion but you don't take chances with their money. So, even though you and I know the changes being made are radical taking them from low risk investment to moderate and high risk investments with a quicker turnaround I make it look like the changes are subtle and minimal. If I can sell this to them and they receive their quarterly statements back showing a sizeable gain on their investment I'll have them eating out of my hand."

"True. True."

"And I guess I've met with three quarters of the firm's larger accounts and they've already see the change so they're staying the course and upping the ante but there are still a few stragglers—you know some non-believers and skeptics. They're a tougher sell but you know me. What's my name?" he said laughing and pouring himself a shot of Chivas and mixing it with. "But enough about work... How was your day?"

"Quiet. I read one of your Donald Goin's novels."

"Oh yeah. Which one?"

"Crime Partners."

"That's the one with Kenyatta if I remember correctly?"

"Yeah that's the one and I really enjoyed it. Goines writes well and is a master storyteller but I was reading the author's bio and it was so interesting that it forced me to go online and find out more. I was shocked to find out that he was a heroin addict for much of his writing career and still managed to write extremely well until he was murdered. It is so sad. And I thought about all the young Black geniuses whose lives are cut short by their addictions. It got me to thinking about Coltrane and Miles."

"Society baby. It's extremely hard out here for a Blackman and then when you posess some talent it's twice as hard."

"But you know they have all these things you here to bring you down. Why would you fall victim knowing they have you destined to fail?"

"Sometimes knowing what' awaits you, though it can be life threatening is still a better remedy than enduring the normal everyday pain of being a Black man in America but enough about that. Let me tell you about a couple of interesting conversations I had today."

 "Please tell me they have nothing to do with work. You know I thought I would miss it but I don't miss it at all."

"I feel you and no it's not about work."

"Go ahead then.

Anthony recounted the conversations with Malik and Syl and for the first time in her pregnancy Samantha picked up the pack of cigarettes she carried in her purse and drew one out. Lighting it she inhaled deeply.

"Do you believe her?"

"I want to but it really doesn't make sense."

"What doesn't make sense?"

"Well, the fact that she seems to be taking the high road and letting the chips fall where they may."

"If that's the case then what's the need for a private investigator?"

"My sentiments exactly," Anthony said shaking his head in agreement. "She's up to something. Of that I'm sure. I just have no idea what it is. I'm going to wait to hear from Malik and see what the private investigator can tell us. I think she's too smart to confide anything in him but you never know."

Samantha sipped her drink casually seemingly engrossed in her own thoughts.

"You now I haven't dated much in my life Anthony but in the two or three times I had the courage to expose my heart I held on tightly and prayed that it would work out in my favor and obviously they didn't or I wouldn't be sitting here with you if they had but never at any time did I wish them any harm or try to cause them pain because shit didn't work out I just chalked it up and took sole responsibility for my part in it not working out. And then I went on with my life. I'm not saying it didn't hurt but life goes on."

"And you told me that why?"

"Because I don't understand why it's so important for her to cause you pain. Why doesn't she just go on with her life? Life is too short to spend time hating and trying to seek revenge."

"You're absolutely right but you have to understand the mentality of the person you're dealing with. If you know Syl like I do then you simply have to chalk it up. Do you know the Serenity Prayer?"

"No."

"It asks that you change the things that you have the power to change and accept the things that you're unable to change. It's that simple. "

"So, you're telling me that the fact that Syl may be trying to sabotage everything that you've ever worked for doesn't bother you."

"I can't afford to let her be a distraction in my life. Syl is doing the only thing she knows how to do and that's to be vindictive. She's very bright but as you know there's a thin line between madness and genius. Syl's very bright but she has some very serious issues. She has trust issues and especially with men. When she was a freshman in college she was going with some football player and he and some friends gang raped her so she has some very serious trust issues when it comes to men. So, you can best believe that after twelve years of getting to know and trust someone she's feeling like the rug has been pulled from under her and is seething about now. I'm almost positive that she has something in the works to bring me down."

"I didn't know."

"I know but I thought it important that you did know and understood that this may take some time to work through. Are you absolutely sure you want to go through this?"

"Baby you should know by now that I'll endure the fires of hell to be by your side."

"That's nice to know but I want you to be on your p's and q's where this is concerned."

"I will babe. You just worry about yourself."

"Always. Any mail?"

"Yes dear. It's on the living room table. I noticed there was a letter from your friend Mr. Dalton. It was torn open when I got it but I didn't read it. I wonder what he wants."

"Hold on and I'll tell you in a minute." Samantha was right. The letter had been tampered with but it didn't matter. The only thing Jonathan Dalton wanted was money he certainly wasn't sending any.

"It's an invitation to see some of his homes out on the island for next Saturday followed by a gathering at his home in South Hampton. You wanna go?"

"I don't know. I've never rubbed noses with the rich and famous. I don't know if I'd fit in."

"About as well as this boy from uptown . C'mon! I think it'll be fun seeing how the other half lives."

"What do you mean the other half? He invited you because you're a part of that half."

"My pockets may say that but my mind will always be with the poor and disenfranchised."

"Oh my knight in shining arm, my Robin Hood, how chivalrous you are," Sammy said snuggling close to Anthony and putting his hand on her stomach. "Can you feel him kicking?"

"A little. So you wanna go?"

"Oh, most definitely."

"Okay then I'll R.S.V.P him."

The weekend served to be like all the rest, quiet and peaceful. Anthony brought his work home with him and went over all of his accounts with a fine tooth comb while Sammy double checked his figures and did the same. When all that was done they sat down and had cocktails and discussed each account in its entirety and the needs of each client. It had been no different in Baltimore on the weekends when Anthony would come to visit. An avid reader Sammy read anything and everything to do with the stock market and brokerage firms. At the end of six months Anthony had to admit that she was ready and as soon as the baby was born and able to go to daycare Sammy would return to work as a junior stockbroker and in two years be promoted to a senior accountant.

In the same time frame she would go back to school via online courses and receive her master's in business dispelling all rumors of nepotism. Anthony already knew Samantha was ready but still had to put her time in. She readily agreed and everything seemed to be falling into place nicely. The future appeared bright for the young couple except for one small factor. Syl was still out there lurking an uneasy calm surrounding her. And despite her acceptance she remained the one variable neither could make go away. And though her name was seldom brought up she instilled a fear in both of them.

Monday was typical but Anthony was fine for the first time in months. His accounts in order he could proceed throwing caution to the wind. He was to meet Sammy for lunch and do a little shopping although he could hardly understand why. She carried well and anyone who didn't know would hardly recognize that she was six months pregnant. Sure those who knew her like mommy and Ant recognized that she had gained a little and that her hips were spreading but most men didn't and continued to hit on her in the usual manner. The fact that she'd gone from a size eight to a healthy twelve only turned Anthony on. What he didn't understand however was her need to shop with the recent wardrobe she'd just been endowed with. Still, he didn't question her when she asked her to join him for lunch and to pick out something for the Dalton affair. So, without further ado he met her at the cute little Mexican she'd come to adore so much since her return to the city. Following lunch he followed her from one Soho boutique to the next until after seven or eight he begged her to find something.

"Baby, I don't think there are any more boutiques in Soho."

"You know, I think you're right. There is one more up on West 4th though."

"Oh my goodness no. What's wrong with that little chartreuse number we saw three boutiques ago?"

"Are you serious? Did you really like that? I didn't take you seriously when you said you liked it."

"I did. You're a knockout and I thought you looked fabulous in it."

"Do you really think so or are you just saying that 'cause you're tired of shopping?'

Anthony laughed.

"No, no. I'm serious I loved the chartreuse."

"Okay, then the chartreuse it is. C'mon let's go."

Leaving the boutique Anthony felt that uneasy feeling he felt ever since he'd left Sylvia. Turning quickly he noticed a rather distinct looking gentleman in a London Fog staring in his direction. There was no doubt the man was following them. Anthony immediately took his cell from his pocket and called Malik.

"Blackman, I'm down here in Soho doing a little shopping with Sammy and I come out of the store and there's this brother standing here watching me."

"'Bout six four, about two hundred, two ten with a black mole on the right side of his face?"

"Yeah, that's the guy."

"Syl's boy. We made him the offer and he rejected it. I think he's trying to push up on her but don't worry about him. I've been meaning to take care of that but I've just been so busy I haven't had a chance to get around to it yet but I'll put that at the top of my list. Don't sweat it Tone you won't see him again."

"I have your word on that Blackman."

"Have I ever failed you my brother."

"Thanks Malik."

"Not a problem."

It didn't make sense. She'd been convincing enough so why was she having him followed? But Malik was true to his word and no longer did he feel threatened or worry about being followed. Saturday arrived with all the peaceful aplomb of Hurricane Katrina. Samantha was still doing her hair at twelve when the chauffer called from downstairs to say he was waiting and Anthony was just now getting into the shower.

"Hurry up honey," Sammy yelled from the bedroom where she sat at the vanity brushing on her mascara.

"Be out in a second. Why don't you run down and tell him to go grab a coffee or something 'til I'm ready."

"I'll do one better. I'll take him a coffee and bagel and let him know that we'll only be a second."

"By the time Anthony got out of the shower Samantha was already back in the loft. Looking at her he smiled.

"My God Sammy, " he said taking her all in. Outfitted in the chartreuse dress and matching heels he gasped at her breathtaking beauty. Her olive skin shone more radiant than it ever had. Anthony smiled. "He may have to wait just a few minutes longer."

Still dripping wet he grabbed her in his arms and kissed her passionately.

"Anthony you're wetting up my dress," she giggled doing her best to push him away. But her resistance did little and she quickly gave in to his advances.

"Baby I love you so much."

"I love you too Anthony."

Letting the towel fall from his waist he pulled her panties down and lifted her dress. Entering her slowly, gently he whispered into her ear.

"Will you marry me tomorrow?"

"Only if you promise me that it will last 'til infinity."

"I promise."

"Til infinity?"

"Til infinity and a day."

A half hour later Anthony and Sammy sat in the back of the chauffeur driven limousine and headed for somewhere out on the island. The atmosphere light, they sat fingers intertwined listening to Sade's Lover's Rock. Minutes later Samantha fell asleep her head resting on Anthony's shoulder and again he smiled. He couldn't remember being happier when the driver pulled over.

"Something wrong boss?" Anthony questioned.

It was then that the driver turned and slid back the dividing window. Anthony was shocked to see the same man he'd seen earlier that week at the boutique. What he saw next was even more shocking as the driver pulled a nine millimeter aimed it at Samantha who remained asleep and fired at point blank range.

"Compliments of Sylvia Pendleton," he said as Anthony cried out in horror. Samantha's blood covered Anthony who was reeling in shock. He turned to look at the gunman and never felt the blast of the gun as the bullets hit tearing away half his face.

"There is no wrath like a woman's was all that could be heard as the gunman got out of the long black limousine and crossed the street to the airport.